"We should probably be getting back to the hotel."

"Go ahead. I need to pack everything up."

Rather than leave her alone in the gathering dark, Shane spent the next twenty minutes helping her extinguish the candles and collect the hurricane lamps.

"Thanks for helping me," Isabel said. "Sometimes romance is a lot of work."

While her jaunty tone gave the statement a lighthearted spin, Shane responded in a serious vein.

"Which explains why I'm single," he said. "What about you?"

"Me?" Isabel gusted out a laugh, obviously uncomfortable having the tables turned on her. "I guess I spend so much time focused on making other people's romantic dreams come true that I neglect my own."

"So you don't practice what you preach?"

"Maybe the right guy hasn't come along."

Shane snorted, thinking how she'd gotten into his head with all her talk of romance. "I think you could make any man the right guy."

"Even you?"

* * *

Taken by Storm is part of the
Dynasties: Secrets of the A-list series.

Dear Reader,

I'm so excited to be part of this Secrets of the A-List series with the wildly talented Karen Booth, Reese Ryan and Joss Wood. We laughed. We cried. But mostly we wrote about four passionate couples leading intertwined lives. I had a blast crafting my story in *Taken by Storm*, which features a free-spirited romance concierge and her workaholic boss. She thinks she's showing him what romance is all about, but he teaches her what it means to fall in love.

I hope you enjoy all four stories, starting with Karen Booth's *Tempted by Scandal*, then my story, *Taken by Storm*, followed by *Seduced by Second Chances* by Reese Ryan and at last *Redeemed by Passion* by Joss Wood.

Happy reading!

Cat Schield

CAT SCHIELD

———

TAKEN BY STORM

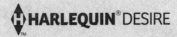
HARLEQUIN® DESIRE

Special thanks and acknowledgment are
given to Cat Schield for her contribution to the
Dynasties: Secrets of the A-List miniseries.

PLEASE RECYCLE

Recycling programs
for this product may
not exist in your area.

ISBN-13: 978-1-335-60369-2

Taken by Storm

Copyright © 2019 by Harlequin Books S.A.

www.Harlequin.com

Cat Schield is an award-winning author of contemporary romances for Harlequin Desire. She likes her heroines spunky and her heroes swoon-worthy. While her jet-setting characters live all over the globe, Cat makes her home in Minnesota with her daughter, two opinionated Burmese cats and a goofy Doberman. When she's not writing or walking dogs, she's searching for the perfect cocktail or traveling to visit friends and family. Contact her at catschield.com.

Books by Cat Schield

Harlequin Desire

Las Vegas Nights

The Black Sheep's Secret Child
Little Secret, Red Hot Scandal
The Heir Affair

Sweet Tea and Scandal

Upstairs Downstairs Baby
Substitute Seduction
Revenge with Benefits

Visit her Author Profile page at Harlequin.com, or catschield.com, for more titles!

You can find Cat Schield on Facebook, along with other Harlequin Desire authors, at Facebook.com/harlequindesireauthors!

To my Desire sisters, Karen, Reese and Joss.
You put the fun in fungo!
It was a joy to work with each of you!

Don't miss a single book in the
Dynasties: Secrets of the A-List series!

Tempted by Scandal by Karen Booth
Taken by Storm by Cat Schield
Seduced by Second Chances by Reese Ryan
Redeemed by Passion by Joss Wood

One

He's Just Not That Into You.

The title of Isabel Withers's favorite rom-com movie and, unfortunately, the theme of her love life. Or lack thereof. In fact, a better title might have been *He Doesn't Know You're Alive.*

The same couldn't be said for Isabel. She was dreamily, frustratingly, sexually, heart-palpitatingly aware every time Shane Adams stepped into The Opulence, a five-star luxury getaway resort an hour east of Seattle. The president in charge of Richmond Hotel Group wasn't just handsome, with his broad shoulders and piercing sable eyes. He wore aloofness like a magical cloak, enthralling Isabel at first sight.

Her movie title would go more like... *He Knows You're Alive, but Only as the Helpful Employee Who*

Drops Everything to Get Him What He Needs in the Hope That He'll Notice the Woman beneath the Uniform.

"You just sighed." This statement came from Isabel's best friend, Aspen Wright.

Isabel shot her a look. "You've been sighing since Richmond announced it was hosting its fifth anniversary retreat here."

With a sly smile that softened the lines of tension around her eyes and mouth, Aspen replied, "I sigh to relieve tension." The creative genius behind the resort's lavish events, Aspen was currently stressed to the nines after Matt Richmond hired A-lister event planner Teresa St. Claire to coordinate Richmond's upcoming retreat. "You're sighing because that chiseled hunk of you-can't-touch-this just walked by."

Aspen was right and Isabel wasted no breath arguing. "I can't help it. He's just so gorgeous."

"That he is. And all business."

Recognizing that Aspen was once again counseling her to give up her crush, Isabel responded with the same stubborn determination that marked her rise from someone who grew up wearing thrift-store clothes to The Opulence's head concierge and self-appointed representative of all things romantic at the resort.

"And that's exactly how I'm going to approach him this time."

"Oh, honey—"

Isabel raised her hand like a determined traffic cop. "Don't." She'd heard Aspen's lecture all too often and predicted what she was about to say. "I just know there's something between us. It's impossible for me to feel as strongly about him as I do and have it be only one-sided."

"Says every stalker ever."

"I'm not a stalker."

"You find ways to run into the man at every turn." Aspen ticked off each point on long, slender fingers. "You know his schedule better than he does. You make sure he has the best table whenever he dines at Overlook and that his room is stocked with all his favorites whenever he stays overnight."

"That's just part of the fine service we offer here at The Opulence," she said, waving away her over-the-top service to their executive. "And why wouldn't we want him to have the absolute best experience every time he comes here? It only improves his perception of the resort."

Aspen shrugged. "Some days I'm not sure he notices any of the positive features we have to offer. He's too busy trying to improve efficiency."

Rigidly organized and driven to improve the resort's already stellar efficiency, Shane was a formidable taskmaster and prone to terrifying the staff whenever he made an appearance. It wasn't that he was harsh with any of his employees, but the man was so focused on business that he simply forgot to smile when things went well.

"He needs someone to soften his edges," Isabel said. "Someone who can show him that the resort's success isn't just about providing consistent service, but that we pour our heart and soul into giving our customers a unique experience."

"Someone like you?"

Hearing the teasing lilt in Aspen's voice, Isabel released a wide grin. "Do you know of anyone better?"

"No," Aspen conceded. "Just don't be disappointed if you fail. I admire everything you've accomplished in the year since you arrived here, but that man's cold heart may be frozen too solid for even your warm touch to heat."

"I'm The Opulence's romance concierge." Isabel lifted her fist in a gesture of power and triumph. "I will not fail in my mission."

A champion of true love, Isabel believed that everyone had the perfect someone out there. Even Aspen, although the older woman scoffed every time Isabel brought the subject up. As for herself, Isabel daydreamed about Shane Adams, even as she recognized that they were opposite in almost every way.

Aspen regarded her with solemn eyes. "Maybe I'll stock up on ice cream and red wine just in case."

Automatically brushing off Aspen's cynicism, Isabel blew her friend a kiss and headed to the little office behind the front desk where she organized romantic events for the guests who came to The Opulence looking to celebrate or connect with their partner. Each experience was tailored to the couple's particular needs and wants thanks to a questionnaire that Isabel had developed over the last few months.

Although she had a degree in hotel management, Isabel's knack for customer service had evolved into a passion for delivering fantasy romance experiences after her first month at The Opulence when a dreamy weekend she'd planned had helped a long-married couple see that their marriage could be saved.

"Fighting for love one couple at a time," Isabel muttered as she settled into her desk chair and pulled up the presentation she'd been working on to convince Shane that they should actively promote The Opulence as a romantic destination.

Satisfied that the pitch had the right balance of facts and fancy to convince Shane this was a solid marketing strategy, Isabel dialed Shane's personal assistant. By the third ring, when Sheila picked up, Isabel's heart was hammering so hard she could barely hear herself ask the question she'd been rehearsing.

"Hi, Sheila, it's Isabel Withers from The Opulence."

"Hello, Isabel." Shane's assistant had a warm, inviting manner so unlike her brisk, all-business boss. "What can I do for you today?"

"I was hoping I could get a meeting with Shane while he's here. I have some ideas for the resort that I'd like to go over with him."

If Sheila found it odd that Isabel would skip over the resort's management and go straight to Shane, she gave no indication. In fact, Isabel had already mentioned her idea to Tom, but he hadn't grasped the value in it. Going over his head was a risk, but if she could convince Shane, the gamble would pay off.

"With the upcoming Richmond event, Shane's schedule is full," Sheila said.

"If you could squeeze me in," Isabel persisted, uncaring that she sounded desperate. "I'll take fifteen minutes. Whatever he can spare." Hell, she was so convinced her idea was a good one she was ready to chase him into an elevator and pitch him on the run.

"Well…" Sheila paused and Isabel could hear the keys clicking on her computer. "He's free for dinner tonight at eight."

Isabel didn't hesitate. "I'll take it." Dinner with Shane? A dream come true. "I'll get us a table at Overlook. Thanks, Sheila."

"I've added you to his schedule. And you're his last meeting of the day, so you won't have to rush."

Was it Isabel's imagination or did Shane's assistant sound as if she was smiling?

"Thanks for your help."

Hanging up with Sheila, Isabel exited the tiny office and made her way back to the concierge desk. The carpet seemed suspended over hundreds of springs because Isabel noticed an extra bounce in her stride. She noted several guests responding to her wide grin with smiles of their own. This only added to Isabel's bright mood.

The concierge currently assigned to the desk looked up from her computer as Isabel approached. "Shane Adams was looking for you a few minutes ago."

Isabel's nerves vibrated in a mixture of alarm and glee. "Did he say what about?"

"He wanted your report on the arrangements for extra activities during the Richmond retreat."

She'd already shared the information with Teresa St. Claire as well as The Opulence management team, but wasn't surprised that Shane Adams had requested the update, as well. He'd been quite hands-on these last few weeks leading up to corporate's massive event. And with good reason. This was a major opportunity to show off the best of the hotel's operation to A-listers and some of the wealthiest people in the country.

Although Isabel knew she could simply send Shane the report by email, she always grabbed any opportunity to speak to him in person. "Did he say where he'd be?"

"He's over there." Cindy pointed toward the front door, where Shane was currently deep in discussion with The Opulence's executive manager, Tom Busch.

As if suddenly aware he was being discussed, Shane glanced toward the concierge desk, and his keen brown gaze struck Isabel, knocking the breath from her lungs. That the man could land such a blow to her senses from clear across a room should've put Isabel's defenses on alert. Instead, she responded with a warm smile that hinted at the strength of her infatuation.

He blinked.

Isabel's heart leaped as his eyes narrowed and he seemed to truly take her in for the first time in a year. This was it. The moment she'd been waiting for. He would see her as a beautiful woman he desired and recognize that she was someone who strove to improve the hotel's reputation every chance she got.

And then it was over. Shane turned his attention back to the executive manager, dismissing Isabel from his thoughts.

She sagged like a leaky balloon.

Moments later, he ended his conversation and she headed his way. Clutched to her chest was the ten-page document detailing every guest's preferences, their requested spa services, rounds of golf, and the schedule of visits to area attractions including the local winery and those participating in unique interactive culinary experiences offered at Quintessential Chef.

"Here's the report you wanted," Isabel said, waiting in breathless silence for several heartbeats while Shane scanned the document.

With his attention focused elsewhere, she took several seconds to drink in the strong structure of his jaw and cheekbones. The ever-present dent between his eyebrows and surprisingly full, kissable lips. She shivered at the thought of how their softness would feel against her skin and wasn't prepared when he lifted his gaze and caught her staring at him.

His eyes narrowed as he silently studied her. Isabel bit her lip to stop herself from babbling out an apology for the infatuation he must've seen written all over her face, but his phone buzzed, interrupting his focus.

"If you have any questions, we can go over them tonight," Isabel said, rushing to make the offer before she lost his attention once more. "I've arranged for a table at Overlook at eight." Isabel barely paused for breath. Shane hadn't yet answered his phone—his gaze hadn't even drifted toward the demanding thing—and she was going to capitalize on every millisecond of his notice. "I'm really looking forward to our dinner."

Heart hammering with uncharacteristic vigor, Shane Adams regarded the plucky redhead standing before him while his phone's insistent buzz barely registered. Striving for detachment and finding it beyond his grasp, he surveyed Isabel's flawless pale skin, the thick dark lashes framing her lively hazel eyes, and her lush mouth painted a rosy pink while her words replayed in his head.

I've arranged a table at Overlook at eight.

I'm really looking forward to our dinner.

Had she just asked him out?

Since Isabel Withers had joined Richmond Hotel Group, he'd noticed a disturbing tendency to become distracted whenever he visited The Opulence. With her russet hair and lively personality a beacon for his attention, he'd pinpointed her as the source of his agitation. But it wasn't until midway through his first quarterly tour, when he caught himself trying to identify what about her perfume had caused him to lean forward and suck in a lungful of the lushly aromatic, sweet scent, that he realized what a danger she was to his disciplined professionalism.

"Ah—" Damn the woman. Her invitation left him gaping at her like an idiot. "I'm not sure my schedule—"

"Oh, don't worry. I already checked with Sheila. She said you were booked into meetings all day, but that you were free after eight. That's why I arranged for a table at Overlook then."

"You spoke to my assistant?"

Shane imagined the glee with which Sheila had fielded that particular phone call. She was constantly harping on him to take a little time out of his schedule to date. Although he never did anything to fix the situation, Shane recognized the need for balance in his life. Working eighty hours a week might not have been a problem for him, but he recognized his staff didn't have his endurance.

"Of course." Isabel's lips parted in a dazzling smile

that made Shane's head spin. "I check with her every time you visit so I can make sure all your needs are met."

His needs?

Those two words sent sexual awareness rushing through him. He barely won the battle to keep his gaze from roaming down her slender frame, but that didn't stop him from speculating about the sort of curves hidden beneath the hotel's blue-and-gold uniform. Shane yanked his thoughts back under control. She was one of his employees. He couldn't go there. Ever.

Shane made a mental note to set up a date in the near future with one of the women he saw from time to time. He'd obviously neglected his *needs* as the Richmond retreat drew near.

He cleared his throat. "Well, I do need to eat," And it was a business dinner. Despite that momentary slip-up, he shouldn't have trouble keeping things strictly professional. "We should discuss the specific arrangements for each of the VIPs arriving next week."

Isabel nodded. "Actually, we have a meeting scheduled with Teresa tomorrow to go over those details. I have something else I'd like to discuss with you."

Something of a business nature? Her expression gave him no clue, but nothing in the last year indicated she was anything other than a professional. With a sinking feeling, he realized his earlier flare of personal interest was leading him to question her motives.

"Can you give me a hint what that might be?"

"I'd rather surprise you." She hit him with another bright smile, this time flavoring it with a dash of sly teasing. "I'd really appreciate if you'd come to dinner with an open mind."

Against his better judgment, Shane found himself utterly intrigued. "Why would you think I'd do otherwise?"

Her eyebrows rose at his question. "You have very strong opinions about everything done at the resort."

Although her measured tone and demeanor remained neutral, Shane recognized the point she was trying to make. He'd shown a heavy hand at The Opulence in the three years following Richmond Hotel Group's management of the resort. The place had been a chaotic mess when they'd won the contract. By instituting strict rules for how everything was done, from folding towels to welcoming the guests, he'd whipped the operations into shape in record time.

The turnaround had been instrumental in boosting him into the presidency of the Richmond Hotel Group division of Richmond Enterprises. He was proud of how the division had flourished with him at the helm. Of course, as more properties had been added to their management portfolio, he'd focused his attention on getting the newer ones up to RHG standards, leaving the earliest properties to function without as much oversight. For most this had worked out well.

Normally Shane didn't weigh in on staffing decisions at the hotel level, but he hadn't liked some of the reports that had been coming out of The Opulence. Tom Busch had been hired by the area manager ten months earlier to act as the hotel's executive manager, and the level of customer service had begun to drop.

The timing of this was not good with the fifth anniversary retreat for Richmond Enterprises taking place in less than two weeks. Everything needed to be running as smooth as glass. The smallest bump could have a catastrophic ripple effect.

"So, we're having dinner to talk about the resort?" he asked.

The shock on her face, quickly masked, sent a flurry of curses winging through his mind. Had he really just admitted to her that he'd assumed her invitation had been personal rather than business?

She gnawed on her lower lip and avoided his gaze. A betraying flush raced up her throat and turned her cheeks bright pink. Shane noticed his own skin becoming hotter with each breath. What was it about Isabel that consistently threw him off balance?

An awkward, breathy laugh escaped her. "Of course. You didn't think I was hitting on you, did you?"

"Well…no," Shane replied, but his response lacked conviction. He cleared his throat, discomfort rendering him less judicious than usual.

"And if I was?" The smile she threw at him had cheeky undertones.

Attraction flared anew, tightening his gut. The unwelcome sensation continued to disturb him. "I always keep my business relationships strictly professional."

"Of course," she repeated, nodding vigorously. "And it isn't as if I thought…" Hot color flushed her cheeks as she trailed off.

It occurred to Shane that this was the longest conversation he'd ever had with Isabel. He was starting to understand why all the management staff remarked on her winning personality as often as they praised her high level of customer service. She had a knack for drawing people in and making them like her.

"I imagine you have a lot of women hitting on you," she prompted when he declined to venture into the silence building between them. "After all, you're handsome, intelligent and successful."

"Not as many women as you think," he lied, easing her tension with a dry smile. "I work too much and play too little. Friends assure me I will end up a crusty old bachelor if I keep going like this."

Why was he discussing his personal life with a member of his staff? Because this slender redhead roused all sorts of unprofessional impulses.

"All it will take is the right woman."

He doubted that was true. "Spoken like a true romantic."

"You say 'romantic' like it's a dirty word."

He used his thumb to gesture at his chest. "Crusty old bachelor."

"You don't believe in romance?"

He was an emotionally shuttered workaholic. "Let's just say I don't have time for it."

"But do you believe in it?" she persisted, mesmerizing him with the specks of green shimmering in her hazel eyes.

"No."

The single, blunt syllable was meant to shut down the conversation. To his dismay, he underestimated the petite idealist. She grinned at him, her challenging smirk a too-late warning that he'd blundered into quicksand.

Before he could elaborate or explain, her smartphone buzzed. She shifted her attention to the screen and sighed.

"The Jamisons' wedding party has started to arrive early and we're not quite ready for them. I have to go. See you at eight." And then she was speeding off, her long strides taking her arresting presence beyond his reach.

In the back of his mind, a voice reminded Shane why he avoided engaging with this woman. All the information he gleaned about her from his management staff said she excelled at her job because she had a knack for reading people and providing them an experience they didn't even realize they wanted. Returning guests flocked to her concierge desk, knowing anything Isabel planned for them would be the perfect experience.

Alone with his thoughts, Shane found himself needing a bracing hit of brisk mountain air. He turned in the opposite direction and headed for a side door that led to the lower terrace. That the encounter had not gone his way didn't surprise Shane. Isabel's quick mind, passionate nature and eloquence were more than a match for his dogged determination and disciplined pragmatism.

He glanced at his watch as a cool fall breeze smacked his overheated face. He had four hours until their next meeting. Barely enough time for him to shore up his defenses. One thing was for certain, he needed his wits about him when dealing with Isabel Withers.

Two

"I can't believe you lied to me."

Teresa St. Claire shied away from the accusations blazing in Liam Christopher's eyes and shifted her attention toward the document clutched in his left hand. His father's will. The venom in his eyes lanced through her, cutting deep into her heart. It was as if every bit of rapport they'd developed these last few weeks had been erased in the time it took for her to use the bathroom.

Five minutes.

What could possibly have gone this wrong in such a short period of time?

When she'd slipped away from the yacht's lounge, he'd been relaxed and in a good mood, his obvious affection turning her bones to mush.

The last thing she expected on her return was to bear the brunt of his cold fury.

"I didn't. I haven't," she insisted, confused and off balance. "What's going on?"

The stack of papers fluttered as he gestured with them. "My father left you twenty-five percent of his personal stock in Christopher Corporation."

He'd done what?

"That's crazy," Teresa murmured, barely able to breathe as she struggled to absorb that his father, her mentor, had left her a small fortune. "I don't understand."

Shock and dismay made her thoughts thick and gummy. Beneath her feet, the sixty-eight-meter yacht churned placidly through the calm waters of Puget Sound, but Teresa's equilibrium pitched and heaved. She tottered over to the closest chair and sat down.

Why would Linus leave me anything?

"…a year?" Liam had continued speaking, but she'd stopped listening. His voice had sounded muffled and indistinct as if she was hearing him while being submerged in water. "I need those shares back now."

The rage in Liam Christopher's voice sliced through the fog surrounding Teresa. Wincing at his fury, she blinked several times to clear her vision. When she glanced his way, she wished his features had remained indistinct.

She held out her hands in a conciliatory manner. "I missed what you said just now about the will's terms. Could you repeat the last part?" She forced a shaky laugh. "This is all overwhelming."

"My father put a clause in the will that states you

can't divest yourself of the shares unless and until you spend a year on the board."

"What?" This additional complication on top of an already tricky situation threatened to overwhelm Teresa's ability to maintain some semblance of calm.

"Seems my father believed you'd be good for our company."

Obviously Liam disagreed.

Anger painted fiery blotches over his cheekbones. With his eyes shooting steel and his jaw locked in stubborn lines, he vibrated with fury. The emotion highlighted his raw masculinity and set Teresa's heart to pounding for all the wrong reasons.

Stop it.

The man was poised to murder her and here she was, swooning over how gorgeous he looked.

"This whole thing is unacceptable," Liam snarled, bringing Teresa's attention back to the real problem. "You don't deserve those shares."

"Maybe not," she declared. *But why did your father want me to have them?*

Liam grabbed the arm of her chair and leaned toward her. "It seems pretty clear to me now that you've been underplaying your relationship with my father all along."

"That's not true," she insisted, sick of defending herself. "Look, I have no idea what Linus was thinking, giving me the shares."

"Don't you?" Liam declared, his voice low and savage.

Teresa ground her teeth together and fought to remain calm. "We did not have an affair." How many times would she have to make this same speech before he believed her?

He's never going to believe me. Just like he's never going to trust me.

The pair of declarations flashed through Teresa's mind like a lightning bolt, revealing the bleak landscape of her doomed relationship with Liam and leaving an afterimage of hopelessness imprinted on her brain.

"You're lying."

Teresa wanted to shriek in frustration and despair. How had they found their way back here again?

"What purpose does it serve me to lie to you at this point?" she asked, even as she recognized the futility of trying to reason with Liam. "Your father made a decision. I don't understand it any more than you do. Before your parents divorced, Linus and I were close, but he was my mentor. Nothing more."

She never would've slept with Liam if she thought he hadn't already accepted this. The disillusionment and melancholy unleashed by Liam's dagger thrust of accusations demonstrated just how right she'd been all those years to put her focus on her career and avoid romantic entanglements. Making her love life a low priority had been the right move all along.

"I'm going to make you give those shares back."

And for a moment she wished giving Liam back the shares would mean he might once again look at her the way he had when they'd made love. When that carefully constructed wall she'd raised around her heart to keep it safe and undamaged had shattered.

"You have a year to try," Teresa responded.

"It's not going to take a year."

Teresa met his eyes. "You can't intimidate me into selling you the stock."

"Selling?" Liam released a harsh laugh. "By the time I'm done with you, you're going to be begging me to take it off your hands."

Shane arrived ten minutes early for his dinner meeting with Isabel, expecting he'd be the first one to the table, only to find she'd beaten him. As the hostess led him to the table, the first thing he noticed was that Isabel had worn her hair down. The shimmering russet curtain spilled over her shoulders in a luxurious wave. Next, he realized she'd exchanged her hotel uniform for something white and lacy.

Bridal.

The impression popped into his head and he ruthlessly banished it before it took root.

"Good evening," he said, settling into the seat opposite her, relieved to see a presentation document placed to the left of his table setting. So, despite her attire, this was a business meeting after all.

"Good evening," she echoed. "Thank you again for meeting with me."

"Of course."

The waiter approached, and Shane glanced at Isabel's glass to see what she was having. The goblet held something clear and fizzy. Curious, but unwilling to ask, he ordered the same. When the drink arrived, he discovered it was plain club soda with a slice of lime.

After ordering dinner, he flipped through the bound document. Her presentation was well organized and brilliantly illustrated with catchy phrases and evocative photographs of beautiful couples enjoying each other at various settings in and around the resort.

"This looks quite thorough," he declared. "But I don't understand why you've come to me with this. Shouldn't you've taken it to Tom?"

"I did, but he wasn't…" Isabel trailed off. For the first time since he'd sat down, she displayed uncertainty. Her brows came together as she collected her thoughts. "That is, he's really good when it comes to the hotel's operations…"

Shane already knew that wasn't completely accurate, but stayed silent while she struggled to make her point without throwing her boss under the bus. As unusual as it was, Shane intended to hear the staff's opinions about the executive director and guessed Isabel would be more forthright than most.

"Anything you say here will remain between us," he assured her, before sitting back and letting her marshal her opinion without coaxing or interference.

"He just doesn't understand the heartbeat of the hotel. I thought maybe that would change as he grew more familiar with the staff and our clientele, but the direction he's gone with the promotions hasn't encouraged people to return." She exhaled in a rush and then chuckled. "That didn't explain things very well, did it?"

She appeared unabashed by her stumble, and Shane found this intriguing. He'd never struggled to communicate his opinions. He simply stated his recommendations, confident that he'd thought the matter through and weighed all options.

Shane decided to table all talk of Tom for the moment. "How do you think we should promote the hotel?"

"As a romantic destination." She flashed a grin that struck him like a fist to the gut.

"What if I told you that Tom is focusing on corporate clients per my direction?"

"Then I'd say I'm here to change your mind."

"How do you intend to do that?"

The flickering candlelight revealed a sudden rush of color in her cheeks. "By showing you firsthand some of the most romantic places The Opulence has to offer."

Her suggestion filled him with mixed emotions. He was an executive of the company that employed her, and while he could justify tonight's dinner as a business meeting, she intrigued him both as a woman he was attracted to and as an individual who challenged his perspective on the hotel.

Retreating to the reason for tonight's dinner meeting, he picked up her presentation and began flipping through it again. "What's your vision for The Opulence?"

"The theme is…" Like a Broadway producer of old, she swept her hand in an arc above her head. *"Romance is the elixir of life."* She beamed at him, utterly convinced of her brilliance. "I think The Opulence is ideally suited as a romance destination, and the staff is ready to provide the perfect getaway experience. In fact, I'm gaining a reputation as a romance concierge."

"What does that mean?"

"You might say I have a knack for giving couples the sort of memorable experiences that they rave about to their friends and family."

"What sort of experiences?"

"Mostly over-the-top romance. I want the hotel to be known as the best destination for a special evening or a first kiss. The covered bridge has been the site of several engagements and wedding ceremonies. And I've lost count of how many people have done photo shoots on the lower trail with the waterfall behind them. We have a first-class spa offering all sorts of luxury treatments geared toward couples. We score big points with honeymooners and people who are celebrating anniversaries."

Isabel's enthusiasm and pride washed over Shane, and he felt a stab of envy. When was the last time he'd felt that sort of passion for his work? He recoiled from the answer. Success was rewarding, but all too often he found himself in an ever-spinning circle of dissatisfaction. What did he have to show for all his hard work except more work and more responsibility? He certainly hadn't made his father proud of him. Nothing would do that. So why did he drive himself so hard?

"Romantic dinners in the Overlook." She gestured around them. "Or private, personalized feasts at Quintessential Chef. Who wouldn't want to come here for a small wedding or a lavish blowout affair?"

Her youthful enthusiasm made him feel ancient and too serious by contrast. It came as a surprise that her liveliness appealed to him. Like a bracing breath of fresh air in the morning. Or a caffeine jolt from a double espresso coffee. Her idealistic smiles and fun-loving ideas invited him to play and dream along with her. The part of him that he'd shut down in order to focus on his career awakened, and he found himself enjoying their exchange. A little too much.

Yet here he was, leaning in, ignoring common sense so he could focus on the woman across from him. Not the employee across from him, he noted as candlelight painted gold highlights in her lustrous red hair and added a mysterious bronze glint in her hazel eyes.

The freckles dusted across her nose gave her a girl-next-door look. Her earnest manner and playful smile buffed smooth the rough edges of his impatience and mellowed him. She moved her hands as she talked, prompting him to wonder: if he grasped them, could she speak?

The thought of touching her made his chest tighten. The sudden pain caused his cautious nature to flare. He shouldn't be thinking about her like someone he wanted to get to know personally. Just like he shouldn't have encouraged her to order the dessert she'd raved about. Even now her tongue flicked out to swipe a smear of chocolate off her lower lip, tempting him to pay the bill and hustle her up to his suite.

Of course he couldn't do that. This was a business dinner, a chance for her to pitch him her ideas. And they were all good ones. Her vision to promote the resort as Instagramable was exactly the sort of fresh idea he liked to see from his employees. He refused to jeopardize his professionalism or his career because she stirred his libido.

But it was more than just lust that she'd aroused. Isabel intrigued him. He admired her business sense even as her fanciful imaginings confounded him. Despite their opposite views, he wanted to hear her opinions even if he disagreed with them.

"I feel as if I've lost you," she said, noticing that his attention had wandered. "You don't believe that The Opulence is the perfect romantic destination."

"The hotel is successful because of its exceptional spa, first-class restaurants and outstanding reputation for events."

"But there's magic here, as well." She studied him for several seconds, her eyes narrowing in keen appraisal. "There's a spot I highly recommend to our couples. I'll just have to prove to you that it's the perfect spot for a romantic first kiss."

Wait. Prove it to him? How?

"You're wasting your time."

Women had been trying to find his softer side—without success—since he was old enough to date. Most of the time he wasn't interested enough in them to want to explore past the surface. Sex was one thing. He believed in satisfying a woman in bed, leaving her breathless and sated before he slid back into his clothes and headed for the door. Lingering to snuggle and exchange confidences only led to attachments and took his focus away from work.

Romance meant tapping into his emotions and he had no intention of going there. He'd been raised by a father who valued hard work above all else and cynically avoided showing any emotion beyond annoyance and contempt for his troublesome son. Shane's mother had died when he was eight. He remembered crying at her funeral and how his father had shut him down, telling him to get over it. His mother wasn't coming back and she wouldn't be proud of him for being such a weakling.

"In terms of romance," he said, "you'll find me a hard sell."

From the expression on her face, he saw his mistake. By declaring he was immune, he'd just thrown down a gauntlet.

"What?" he demanded, anxiety and excitement blinking awake inside him.

Her delightful smile took up the challenge. "This is going to be interesting."

Following the bombshell of his father leaving Teresa shares of Christopher Corporation stock, Liam had traded several texts with Matt Richmond, but hadn't yet gotten his best friend on the phone to spill all that had happened regarding his father's will. Because of their similar fortunes and lifestyles, Matt had become someone Liam felt comfortable talking to about business as well as personal issues he might be having.

Which was why Liam wished he had his friend around to talk to about his chaotic emotions where Teresa was concerned. Instead, Matt was unreachable after deciding to extend his quick trip to the Big Apple into a romantic getaway to a destination unknown. Liam didn't want to envy Matt. The Richmond Enterprises CEO deserved to be happy. But Liam couldn't stop comparing his own failed love life to Matt's happy one and wishing he had better luck with women.

Why had Linus given Teresa shares when he could've bequeathed an equally generous amount in cash or property? Hell, if his father had given her the winery and villa in Tuscany, the yacht moored in the Cayman Islands and the vacation house in Bali, Liam might've been furious, but he could've let those things go and wiped Teresa St. Claire from his mind.

Instead, Linus had made it so that Teresa couldn't divest herself of the shares without giving a year of her time to the company's board. The ridiculous codicil put Liam in an untenable position of having to work side by side with a woman he didn't trust.

A woman he desired.

Someone who made him second-guess his perceptions about what he'd believed all his life. Someone who made him question his mother's stories about her failed marriage.

He'd opened himself up to the idea that the connection he felt toward Teresa might have potential. So he'd arranged to spend a perfect evening with her on the yacht. Expensive champagne, a gourmet dinner. A heartfelt apology over how he'd been so suspicious of her. All so he could set the stage for a romantic invitation to stay with him during the Richmond retreat. At the same time, he wanted Teresa there while he read the will, knowing it would be emotional.

He hadn't taken the step lightly. The move would reveal that she was important to him. That he trusted her. All that went up in smoke after the shocking discovery of his father's bequest. While Liam had been falling for her, she'd been lying to him. She'd played him for a fool, and it was long past time for Liam to accept that her innocent act was exactly that.

He'd believed her when she'd claimed that her relationship with his father had been strictly professional, but Linus's gift of twenty-five percent of his shares in Christopher Corporation told a different story.

And demanded further investigation.

His phone rang as he slid behind the wheel of his car. Liam sent his attention flickering toward the screen, where his mother's face had appeared. Ever since his father's death, Catherine Dupont—she'd returned to her maiden name after the divorce—had been avidly curious about her ex-husband's will. She'd received a significant settlement at the time of their divorce, but as Christopher Corporation continued to flourish and grow, she'd resented that her financial situation remained stagnant while Linus grew wealthier by the day.

"Why didn't you tell me you'd heard from your father's lawyer?" Catherine scolded him as soon as he'd greeted her.

Liam wondered how she'd found out. He'd been dodging her for nearly a week, still processing the document's shocking revelation, and wasn't prepared to deal with his mother's reaction when she heard what happened or to explain what his father had done.

"I've been busy." Liam wished he had a better excuse.

"And?" Catherine demanded, not waiting for her son to respond before launching into her interrogation. "Did Linus leave you everything? Of course he did. I suppose he gave something to that secretary of his. She was too territorial for my taste, calling him at all hours with some excuse or another. I'm pretty sure she was in love with him. He was obviously flattered by all her attention. How much did he leave her?"

His mother's rapid-fire questions battered Liam, taking his irritation to new heights. He opened his mouth, determined to shut her down, only to realize that as weary as he'd grown of her suspicious and jaded view of the world, she'd been right to suspect something was going on between Linus and Teresa. This revelation took the edge off his temper toward his mother. Obviously she was right to assume the worst of people.

Yet even as he accepted this, a familiar darkness settled over his mood.

The time he'd spent with Teresa, making love to her, helping her when she freaked out about her brother. That had all been real. Hadn't it? Liam blew out a breath. In the span of a few short minutes, his entire world had gone topsy-turvy. Or maybe it was more the case that his ship had righted itself. Maybe his growing feelings for Teresa had been the anomaly. There was no question he'd felt less like himself over the last few weeks than ever before.

"Liam," his mother said impatiently. "Are you still there? Did you hear what I asked? Did your father leave money to his secretary?"

She never referred to Esther Smithers by her name.

"I'm not sure," he replied, barely remembering anything after the bombshell news that Teresa had received shares that should've been his.

"What do you mean you're not sure?" Her outrage

came through loud and clear. "How can you not be sure? Didn't you read the will?"

"I didn't get a chance to read through the entire thing," he lied. He'd examined every word.

"Why not?"

"He left twenty-five percent of his shares in Christopher Corporation to Teresa St. Claire," Liam blurted out. He gave his mother a heartbeat to absorb the information before continuing, "Any idea why he might've done that?"

"To punish me, obviously."

Her answer was so ridiculous that Liam almost laughed. The only person damaged by Linus's last-minute decision to change his will was Liam. Not to mention his parents had been divorced for a decade. Yet he wasn't surprised that his mother continued to blame Teresa for some nonexistent affair. Catherine Dupont was incapable of letting go of any slight she'd ever received, real or imaginary.

Yet in this instance, his mother could be right about Teresa. Not that she'd had an affair with Linus. Weeks earlier Liam had accepted that she'd spoken the truth about that. But with his passion for her no longer muting his doubts about her, the voice at the back of his mind questioned if he'd missed something equally sinister about their connection.

Obviously more had gone on between them than just a simple mentor/mentee relationship. Had Linus given her the shares because she'd been blackmailing him? Maybe they hadn't slept together, but could he have stepped across the line in the early days of the relationship? Given the enormity of what she'd inherited from his father, it seemed realistic that she'd manipulated Linus somehow.

He made a note to call his private investigator and get the man to focus on his father and what skeletons might have been in his closet that Teresa could've exploited. But first, he needed to disengage himself from the woman railing in his ear.

"Mother," he interrupted when she paused for a rare breath. Honestly, the woman had the lungs of an opera singer. "I need to make some calls. I will check in with you later."

And then, before she could launch into more of her vitriolic spin, he disconnected the call. He had plans to make regarding Teresa St. Claire. Once his strategies were set in motion, it wouldn't matter what she said or did in an effort to sway him. No amount of sexual chemistry or manipulation of his emotions to elicit his sympathy would stop him from recovering what was rightfully his.

Three

In the days following her dinner with Shane, Isabel manned the concierge desk with more than her usual good spirits. Unaffected by the gray skies and sporadic rains that plagued the area or the escalating tension felt by the staff as the Richmond anniversary retreat neared, Isabel hummed and grinned as she went about her day. How could she be anything other than gloriously happy? Not only had Shane been intrigued by her presentation, but also she had the distinct sense that she'd piqued his interest in a way that wasn't solely professional.

Something about the way he lingered after walking her to her car, as if he'd been reluctant for the evening to end, left her wondering if her flirting had gotten to him. What would he do if she leaned in and kissed him? Even as a delicious thrill chased up her spine, she recognized that he'd resist. He wasn't the type to make a pass at one of his employees. Too many scruples. But if she didn't work for him? Would he still rebuff her? The question preoccupied her as she awaited his return to the hotel that afternoon.

"Good afternoon," he intoned, his deep voice sending delicious shivers racing over her skin.

"Hi." She sounded breathless and silly, but he didn't seem to notice. "Are you ready to feel the romance?"

He didn't sigh, but his expression shifted into skeptical lines. "I'm ready to take your proof under advisement."

"Then let's go."

As with every time she drew within ten feet of the man, Isabel's pulse started behaving erratically. She glanced at Shane as they crossed the lobby. His distant expression made her sigh. He had no idea the sort of effect his height and powerful build coupled with his aloof manner had on the people around him. Or maybe he did and just didn't care.

"What's in the bag?" Shane eyed her tote as they emerged into the November afternoon.

"You'll see." Withholding information from him was a risk. The tactic either whetted his appetite or annoyed him. In fact, it was hard to tell how he was reacting. The man was always in control and she despaired of ever knocking him off balance.

In truth, she appreciated the repressed tension that vibrated in him. Like he was a powder keg set to explode any second. What would it take to ignite him?

Would she survive the blast? Get to keep her job? Score the sex of a lifetime?

Isabel tried to match Shane's sedate stride, but her eagerness meant that most of her steps were on the balls of her feet. She moved like a small child eager to get to an ice cream truck, anticipating the joy of a treat on a hot day.

"There are several areas around the hotel that just scream 'kiss me,'" Isabel said, playing tour guide as she led the way toward the trail that wound beside the river above the falls. "The place I'm taking you is my favorite."

After several days of gloomy and damp weather, the sun had poked out in the afternoon to highlight the fiery gold and orange of the autumn mountain foliage. The intermittent rains had soaked the earth and awakened the bracing scent of pine. Through the trees came the distant roar of Centennial Falls. Isabel listened to the steady crunch of their footsteps on the gravel path and noted the calm that settled over Shane as he sucked in a deep breath and let it out.

"There something about the air in the mountains, isn't there?" Isabel asked, unable to maintain her silence. "I'm glad the rain has finally stopped."

She winced at her inane conversational feint. Was she seriously discussing the weather with Shane?

"I've never spent this much time up here," he admitted.

No doubt he had larger, flashier properties that demanded his attention. Although known for its high-end luxury, The Opulence's rustic location made it more like a retreat or getaway destination.

"I really appreciate you driving up to meet with me today."

"Not a problem. I'll be making visits every day between now and the Richmond retreat next week."

"Of course." She tried not to let her disappointment show. Had she really thought he'd make a special trip up here just to meet with her? "Here we are."

The trail led to a covered bridge that spanned the river fifty feet before the top of the falls. It was a magical spot for couples, and Isabel had set the stage to prove it.

"This is your romantic spot?" he peered at the weathered wood structure doubtfully.

Isabel reached into her tote and pulled out two lighters, extending one to Shane. "You'll see what I mean when we're done."

Earlier she'd brought out dozens of hurricane lanterns and filled them with white candles. As the light faded, muting the shocking orange and brilliant yellow trees and deepening the cloudless sky to a rich cornflower blue, the setting would make a gorgeous shot.

Each took one side of the bridge and worked in companionable silence to light candle after candle. Some had been hung by chains from the rafters. Others sat on the railing or the ground. By the time they were finished, the glow of those flickering points of light filled Isabel with warm satisfaction.

"Okay, I'll admit this sets the stage," he said as he handed back the lighter.

Isabel tore her gaze from the covered bridge bathed in flickering candlelight and peered at Shane. He didn't sound like the stiff businessman she'd come to know. He shifted his attention away from her, but not before she saw grudging respect and understanding in his dark brown eyes.

Isabel wrapped her fingers around the tote bag's strap in order to keep from reaching out and touching him. If he was inspired by the romantic scene, then she'd done her job. Few could possibly be as dispassionate as this man beside her. Or maybe *dispassionate* wasn't the right word. Maybe *closed off* would be a better description. He claimed he didn't believe in romance. Perhaps his issue was that he didn't believe in love. Or was he merely afraid to give it a chance?

Had he been hurt by a woman? She found it hard to believe that anyone who'd penetrated Shane's shields could possibly want to hurt him. In a flash of insight, she perceived fragility beneath his take-charge attitude. Was that even possible? How could she imagine Shane being soft or breakable? The man was a slab of granite. Immovable. Unknowable.

"You feel the potential for romance, don't you?" Isabel probed. "The magic of this place that might prompt you to sweep a woman into your arms and kiss her."

"I'm not going to kiss you," he declared, his resistance clearly palpable.

"Of course you're not," she replied breezily. "You're my boss's boss's boss and that would be inappropriate." Her smile grew predatory. "But put that aside for a second and imagine there's something between us. Something that's worth exploring."

"I really can't."

"You want to make a huge impression on me and after hearing that the Overlook has fantastic cuisine and a stellar wine cellar, you decided to bring me up here for a delicious dinner. We share a decadent dessert and with the taste of chocolate on our tongues, we walk hand in hand to this spot."

Moving deliberately, she pressed forward, unsurprised when he retreated. She backed him up against the railing. Eyes narrowing, he made no protest even when her body stopped a few inches from his.

"My heart is racing. I'm tingling all over in anticipation of our first kiss." Her bold declaration caused him to raise his eyebrows.

He cleared his throat. "Okay, I get your point."

"We stop in the middle of the bridge and watch the first stars appear in the sky. You step in close." She seized the railing on either side of his waist, boxing him in.

"It's a very romantic spot." His voice had taken on a husky tenor. That was progress. "I concede that it's beautiful here and perfect for lovers."

Although Isabel had satisfied her purpose in coming here tonight, she was greedy for more. "You cup my cheek in your hand and whisper how you've been waiting all evening for this." She skimmed her fingers across his shoulder and slid her nails through his short hair. "I can't breathe. My knees are going all wobbly. We're alone in the flickering candlelight and you put your arms around me…"

She cleared her throat meaningfully and he exhaled as if in surrender. A second later his hands circled her waist. At first his grip was neutral, neither pulling her in nor pushing her away. Just indulging her bit of play-acting. But as she leaned into him, his fingers tightened almost imperceptibly.

"And I give you a clear signal that I want you to kiss me."

She tugged his head down and lifted onto her toes to bring their lips in close proximity, stopping at the brink. This had to be his move. His choice. She could kiss him and no doubt he'd let her, but she needed him to want her. To be in this moment. To choose her. To step across that line.

"Isabel." Regret filled every syllable.

She tamped down her disappointment and reminded herself that she hadn't brought him here to seduce him. Not exactly. "Tell me you feel the romance," she murmured, letting none of her regret show.

His breath flowed across her lips as he sighed. "I feel it."

And in that moment, it was enough. Isabel eased away and tension flowed out of him.

"If I can get to you," she said, her confidence slowly refilling as she realized his hands continued to span her waist, "I can get to anyone."

She stepped back, conscious how fast the heat beneath her skin began to cool as soon as he stopped touching her.

"I'm not sure if it's the place or if it's you," he grumbled.

Her heart expanded in her chest, making it hard to

breathe. "Come on," she told him, reining in her delight. "It's almost time. We have to go hide."

Hide? Hide where? And why?
Damn it! What had just happened?

Shane ground his teeth, recognizing that he'd let this ridiculous situation go on far too long. The dense woods on either side of the river lent a sense of privacy to their surroundings. He'd been lured into a mellow mood by the tranquil setting, the flickering glow of the candle-light and her inventive narration. Too late he realized that she'd ambushed him. And he'd almost kissed her. That would've been a mistake. A big one.

"Come on," Isabel said, taking his arm and tugging him in the opposite direction from which they'd come.

"Where are we going?" He demanded, pushing impatience into his voice. Silent curses filled Shane's mind. It was hard to resist her. "The hotel is the other way."

"There's something else you need to see."

Their footsteps thumped on the wood as they crossed the bridge and entered the forest on the other side. She tugged him into the shadow of a large pine tree.

"It's getting too dark to see anything."

This wasn't at all what he'd expected out of today's visit. Or was he just kidding himself? He'd studied her proposal and found it reasonable. He'd already decided to circumvent Tom Busch and let her work directly with the marketing department.

He could've just called her with the news. Instead, he was skulking around in the woods with the feisty redhead. To his amazement, despite the ridiculous situation he found himself in, he discovered he was intrigued.

"Can you please tell me what's going on?"

"Just be patient for a few more minutes and all will be revealed."

A slight breeze blew the aroma of pine and damp earth across his face. He filled his lungs with the cleansing air and found himself drawing in her perfume, as well. The intoxicating fragrance relaxed him.

"I really don't have time for this," he complained, but it was a feeble protest.

What was this woman doing to him? He was lurking in the woods, waiting for who knew what to happen. She'd taken his discipline and stubbornness and transformed it into curiosity and excitement until all he wanted was to be on this adventure with her.

"Can you at least give me a hint?"

"I set this up yesterday," she whispered, her entire body vibrating with excitement. "The candles. The perfect spot."

"What's going to happen?" Even as he asked the question, a couple came toward the bridge from the opposite side of the river.

"Here they come." Isabel reached into her seemingly bottomless tote bag and pulled out a camera with an enormous lens. It was the sort of thing sports and wildlife photographers might use.

"Are we spying on someone?" Despite his growing frustration, Shane pitched his voice low to match hers. "Is this something that could damage the hotel's reputation?"

"No, of course not."

"Why do you have the camera?"

"Don't be silly."

He was being silly?

"Then why…?"

"To capture it all, of course."

He didn't see how. The light was fading fast and the numerous candles barely pushed back the shadows beneath the covered bridge. "Capture what?"

"You'll see."

Biting back another demand for answers, Shane focused on the couple. It was obvious from the woman's body language as she caught sight of the candlelit bridge that she was delighted. Beside him Isabel peered through the camera's viewfinder. Caught up in the moment, Shane watched as the man took her hands and walked backward into the flickering light.

His heart gave a funny little jerk. They were both so obviously into each other. What would that be like, he wondered, to give himself completely over to another person? His heart gave a hard yank when the man deposited a tender kiss on her lips before dropping to one knee before her. Her hands went to her mouth and she practically vibrated with excitement.

Although he and Isabel stood too far away to hear what the man had to say, it was pretty obvious what was going on and that the answer to the man's question was a definite yes.

Beside him Isabel grinned and snapped picture after picture, capturing the entire romantic event. With a sigh, Isabel lowered the camera and shot him a wry glance.

"Is this your first proposal?"

"Yes."

"What'd you think?"

"Okay, I get it," he muttered ungraciously. "This is a very romantic spot."

"Come on."

To Shane's dismay, as soon as it appeared as if the couple was done with their private moment, Isabel headed in their direction.

"Congratulations," she called as she approached. "That was the most romantic proposal I've ever seen."

Shane trailed after her, wondering if that was an exaggeration. As he closed the distance, he realized he recognized the newly engaged woman. He'd dated Kendall Chase for a year before she'd ended things, complaining that he was married to his career. And in typical Shane Adams fashion, he'd justified the breakup by throwing himself even harder into work.

Keeping busy distracted him from dwelling on how much he'd liked Kendall. Or from pondering if he'd been in a different place in his life whether he might've married her. She was perfect for him. A lawyer with a large, successful Seattle law firm, determined to make partner, she'd worked incredibly long hours. Well matched in their professional lives until her younger sister and best friend got engaged. After that Kendall started asking Shane hard questions about how he saw their future together and it became pretty obvious that they weren't going to make it.

That was two years ago. Obviously she moved on to someone who suited her better. Someone who could love her and wanted to spend the rest of his life with her. Seeing her happiness, Shane felt a hard lump form in his chest.

"This is all so amazing." Kendall wrapped her arms around her fiancé and gazed up at him adoringly. "I had no idea you could be so romantic."

"I had help." Her fiancé grinned at Isabel.

"Hi, Kendall. I'm Isabel Withers, the hotel's concierge. On behalf of The Opulence, I want to congratulate you on your engagement."

While the happy couple beamed, Shane wondered if Isabel had known about his past connection to Kendall. If she'd invited him to witness this event, intending to rub his nose in his romantic failure.

A quick glance at Isabel made him realize how ridiculous he was being. She was completely focused on the newly engaged couple. Her open and exhilarated expression demonstrated just how deeply committed she was to creating these romantic moments and then being there to watch the magic happen. Making people happy was her mission. And she was damned good at it.

Coming up to stand beside the concierge, Shane offered his own congratulations. As he shook the man's hand, he realized Kendall hadn't noticed him yet. Would she be as shocked to see him at her proposal as he was to be here?

"This is Shane Adams," Isabel said. "He's president of Richmond Hotel Group. They manage the hotel."

"Nice to meet you," Glenn said, but his greeting was drowned out as the woman beside him spoke up.

"Shane Adams?" Kendall blinked as if awakening from a wonderful dream, and her gaze shot in Shane's direction.

Her odd tone caused her fiancé to glance her way. "Do you know each other?"

From his question, Shane gathered Kendall hadn't mentioned him.

"We dated for a while," Kendall said, her tone indicating that period of time was a vague memory, inconsequential and forgettable. "That was over two years ago. I can't believe you're here. Now."

Shane cleared his throat. "Isabel brought me along today because she has this idea that we should promote The Opulence as a romance destination and wanted me to see firsthand what she was talking about."

Isabel's wide eyes as she watched the exchange demonstrated to Shane that the whole situation was one massive, awkward coincidence. "Let's get a few formal shots before you two head to the Overlook for dinner. Something that you could share with your family and friends on social media. I captured several of the actual proposal, but those were for you."

The couple agreed, and Isabel expertly maneuvered them into place and snapped pictures with the candlelight illuminating their happy faces and images of their hands together with her new diamond ring. Shane stepped back to watch it all, noting his appreciation of the way Isabel mixed professional customer service with romantic fantasy. The whole thing was accomplished in less than fifteen minutes and the couple was thrilled with the results. This convinced Shane that Glenn and Kendall—thanks to all Isabel's subtle salesmanship— would return in a year's time to tie the knot.

"Congratulations to both of you," Shane said. "I hope you'll be very happy."

While the couple walked away, Isabel spent several seconds going through the photos on her camera. When enough time had passed for them to be out of earshot, she glanced up at him.

"Was it weird watching your ex-girlfriend get engaged?"

"A bit," he admitted, feeling something unraveling inside him. "I'm glad she found somebody who suited her."

"Were you in love with her? I'm sorry. I shouldn't have asked that. It's too personal."

"I never gave the relationship a chance. She broke up with me because I worked too much."

"Was she in love with you?"

Shane blew out the candle nearest him. "We should probably be getting back to the hotel."

"Go ahead. I need to pack everything up."

Rather than leave her alone in the gathering dark, he spent the next twenty minutes helping her extinguish the candles and collect the hurricane lamps. Isabel fetched the wagon she'd hidden, and, working in silence, they loaded everything into boxes.

Although Isabel hadn't pursued an answer to her earlier question, Shane couldn't stop his churning thoughts. He'd never encouraged Kendall's emotional attachment to him. And even as she'd probed whether they had a future, he suspected if he'd proposed she wouldn't have agreed to marry him.

"Thanks for helping me pack up," Isabel said, her gratitude enveloping him like a soft blanket on a chilly night. "Sometimes romance is a lot of work."

While her jaunty tone gave the statement a lighthearted spin, Shane responded in a serious vein.

"Which explains why I'm single," he said. "What about you?"

"Me?" Isabel gusted out a laugh, obviously uncomfortable having the tables turned on her. "I guess I spend so much time focused on making other people's romantic dreams come true that I neglect my own."

"So you don't practice what you preach?"

"Maybe the right guy hasn't come along."

Shane snorted, thinking how she'd gotten into his head with all her talk of romance. "I think you could make any man the right guy."

"Even you?"

For several seconds he didn't know what to make of her question. They weren't in the least bit compatible. While he admired her for being hardworking, organized and professional, beneath her impeccable hotel uniform beat a fanciful, fun-loving heart he couldn't begin to relate to.

So why did he pause to considered how to answer? And why did his blood course hot and thick through his veins? Too late he realized she was flirting with him. Yet with his heart thundering in his chest, he locked his gaze with hers. Was the overwhelming urge to put his arms around her a trick of the starlight reflected in her eyes?

He cupped her cheek and slid his thumb over her lower lip. Her breath hitched even as his lungs stopped altogether. Madness. He couldn't do this. She was an employee. Completely off limits.

A groan broke loose from her chest, snapping his fraying restraint. Letting his eyes slide shut, he brought his lips to hers. The first kiss he dusted across her incredibly soft mouth, offering her the opportunity to come to her senses. To pull back. To shove him away. She didn't.

To his joyful regret, she leaned into him, pushing up on her toes and driving her lips hard against his. The second kiss escalated fast. While their mouths fused and teeth raked, her fingers combed through his hair, before digging into his skull.

His thoughts became blurry and unreachable as he banded his arm around her waist. Shane slid his other hand into her hair, disrupting the pins holding her updo in place. Curling his fingers around her long, wavy locks, he tugged, changing the angle of her head. She gasped in delight as his tongue slid into her mouth. She welcomed him with a throaty moan that unleashed his desire.

He was on fire for her. A living torch. No longer a cold, dispassionate rock. But an inferno of hunger and lust. The sheer strength of his reaction shocked him into breaking off the kiss. But instead of setting her free amongst a litany of apologies and excuses, he set his cheek against her temple and sucked in several breaths of the chilly mountain air. Her arms went around his waist in a tight hug that he read as affection rather than passion.

A moment later she pushed herself away and raked her fingers through her disheveled hair. She stared at him in wide-eyed amazement for a brief moment before succumbing to an irrepressible grin.

"See," she began, her smoky voice at odds with the delight dancing in her hazel eyes. "I told you. This is the perfect spot for a first kiss."

Four

After yet another mostly sleepless night spent tossing and turning, dawn found Teresa sipping French press coffee at her condo's breakfast bar. She watched rain strike the glass door leading out to her tiny balcony with its peekaboo glimpse of the Sound while her mind replayed last week's shocking revelations on a continuous loop.

She'd contacted Linus's lawyer and confirmed that she now owned a stake in Christopher Corporation. Seven years earlier Linus had been her mentor. Intelligent and successful, kind and encouraging, his advice and guidance had been instrumental in laying the groundwork for what had become Limitless Events.

And if she was honest with herself, her affection for him wasn't solely professional. Teresa had lost her father at a very young age. Could she really be blamed for seeing Linus as a father figure? He'd certainly treated her like the daughter he'd never had. Unfortunately, she'd learned from Liam their closeness had been misinterpreted and created problems with Linus's family. Even though she hadn't realized at the time that she'd been the catalyst for his marriage falling apart, Teresa had limited contact with Linus in the years that followed because she was so focused on becoming successful.

Which made his substantial gift to her so much more shocking. While she wanted to get swept up in joy and wonder at the unbelievable upturn in her fortune, the news dealt a fatal blow to the promising new beginning she and Liam had made. She never should've stepped across the line and fallen prey to her passion for the charismatic Seattle billionaire. Doing so had left her open to being damaged by his distrust and bad opinion.

Dwelling on problems she couldn't begin to fix filled Teresa's anxiety well to the top. With only a week until the Richmond anniversary extravaganza was set to begin, dozens of details awaited her attention. Teresa headed into Limitless Events's offices to check in with her staff. Despite having worked closely with most of them on numerous projects, Teresa had a tough time relinquishing control.

She'd never known if this was something she'd learned during the years she'd trained with Mariella Santiago-Marshall of MSM Event Planning or if it had started in childhood. Teresa's mother had been scattered and overwhelmed by the world even before her husband died. It grew so much worse once Talisa had been left alone to raise her two small children. Teresa had grown up too fast, taking care of both her mother and her baby brother.

"Good morning," Teresa said breezily to Corrine, sailing past the mostly empty desks on her way to her office at the back. "I'd like the status meeting to start in fifteen minutes."

That afternoon she was heading to the hotel where the retreat would be taking place and staying there until the event was done. The Opulence was a one-of-a-kind resort perched on a cliff beside a one-hundred-thirty-foot waterfall with sweeping panoramic views of the river and mountains.

"I sent Martha out for treats," Corrine called after her. "I figured we could all use a sugar rush right about now."

Affection rose in Teresa for her efficient assistant. "Good thinking."

Ignoring the couch where she and Liam had made love for the first time, Teresa settled into her desk chair and set up her laptop. Today the soothing ritual of arranging her phone, notepad, pen and coffee cup in a neat line wasn't having its desired effect. Usually creating order forced her to concentrate on what she could control and calmed her.

Confidence swelled in Teresa as she looked over her to-do lists. This she could handle. This she was good at. Being creative and organized.

She noted the employees assigned to various outstanding tasks and noted which giveaway items still needed to be collected. Each attendee would receive a fabulous gift bag filled with the sort of over-the-top luxury items that A-listers took for granted. She'd also suggested to Matt Richmond that they fill the attendees' suites with flowers and welcome baskets. In some cases they'd tailored the goodies to the guests' particular preferences or dietary concerns, utilizing the hotel's excellent concierge, Isabel Withers, to gather information on each person.

Because the people invited to the Richmond retreat were some of the richest people in the world and Matt insisted that each received personalized attention, Teresa had arranged to bring in additional support staff to cater to their every need.

For the first time she noticed the message light blinking on her phone. Her nerves jangled as Liam's betrayed expression filled her thoughts. Although the message could be one of a hundred different things, she greedily hoped Liam had reconciled himself to not blaming her for his father's bequest and was reaching out to let her know.

If Liam chose to blame her for his father's decision to leave her the stock, nothing she could say would convince him otherwise. It would help if she had a genuine answer that would satisfy him, but when she didn't understand Linus's motivation, how could she make a convincing argument?

The corners of her lips drooped as she pondered her hopeless situation with Liam. She couldn't visualize a path back to a place where he trusted her again. Here was a perfect instance where she had no place to turn for help. The Fixer, the man she'd leaned on in the past, certainly couldn't make this right. How did one go about fixing someone else's broken heart?

Was she heartbroken?

Teresa shied away from the emotional question and focused on a concrete issue instead. As much as Liam wanted the shares of his company back, according to the terms of the will, they were stuck with each other for a year.

She was paralyzed at the idea of having to confront his displeasure for the next twelve months while her own treacherous emotions kept replaying memories of their lovemaking.

What if she refused the shares? Would that enable Liam's faith in her to bounce back?

On the other hand, such a large amount could weatherproof her business against future troubles. She'd be a fool to wager her financial security on a long-shot chance that she could have a future with Liam. There was no guarantee that her sacrifice would bring her a happily-ever-after. Those few glorious times she had spent with Liam had obviously been an anomaly.

Sure, they were sexually attracted to each other, but did either of them have what it took to go the romantic distance? Heaven knew she had a poor track record when it came to intimacy and relationships.

Liam was interesting and irresistible, a combination she found unexpected and intoxicating. He appealed to her mind, body and soul. It was just her luck that so many obstacles stood between them.

Teresa gave an exasperated sigh. She shouldn't waste time bemoaning her past decisions. That's not how she operated her business. It shouldn't be how she handled her personal life. When a problem came up with a client, she took care of the situation, making it right. That sort of confidence didn't follow her into her private life. Like when her brother had been in a jam, she'd reluctantly reached out to the Fixer, thinking the situation beyond her ability to solve. She should've known that someone who took care of problems for the wealthy and elite would expect more than she could afford to pay. And now she owed the man a favor. She shivered with foreboding.

Beyond the tall windows, the gray skies had darkened, making nine in the morning feel more like dusk, matching Teresa's grim mood. She flipped on her desk light and studied the to-do list she'd created that morning, frowning at item five: "Meet with Aspen Wright at two." The hotel's event planner had not appreciated having to take a backseat role with regard to the retreat and had argued with Teresa's decisions at nearly every turn.

Teresa glanced up as several of her staff entered the office, chattering good-naturedly among themselves. At least her staff was upbeat.

The blinking red light continued to demand her attention.

Teresa picked up the handset and dialed her voice mail. The male voice recorded at two that morning wasn't Liam, but her brother Joshua.

"Hey, sis," he said, sounding distracted. Syllables blurring together, he continued. "You're always working so I thought you might be at the office. I need to talk."

To her intense annoyance, the call ended. Questions

buzzed through her mind as she hung up the phone. Had he been cut off? Was he in trouble? Was he drunk? Or drugged? He'd claimed he had his "situation" under control. Was that still the case or had he been overly confident in his ability to fix things?

She dialed his phone and rolled her eyes when she was immediately directed to his voice mail. As she muttered curses while his voice directed her to leave a message after the beep, Teresa's thoughts went back to Linus's final gift to her. Though moments earlier she'd pondered refusing it, she might just need the inheritance to get her brother out of trouble. Again.

Which killed any hope of reconciling with Liam. Maybe as painful as it was to give up on him, that was what was best for her. Chances were his trust issues would've ended up breaking her heart.

Then she noted the ache in her chest. Thought about her sleepless nights.

Maybe it was already too late.

Isabel was sending a confirmation email finalizing details for a party of eight that evening at Quintessential Chef when a furious woman in a glittering designer wedding dress stormed into the lobby from the side terrace. The entire wedding party trailed after her in miserable silence.

"You are useless." The focus of the woman's fury was a slender man with a camera. "My entire wedding will be ruined because you haven't gotten a single decent shot."

Predicting there would be bloodletting soon, Isabel

raced to intercede. The bride was a stunning twenty-eight-year-old blonde from California with nearly four million followers on YouTube and three million on Instagram. She'd started out five years earlier sharing her thoughts, aspirations and daily inspiration surrounding makeup, food, travel and fashion and parlayed her style into a multimillion-dollar business.

None of her charm or signature confidence was in evidence at the moment. She shook with impatient annoyance.

Isabel boldly stepped between the blogger and the embattled photographer. Although Isabel had briefed the photographer on all the best spots to shoot, the man had obviously not paid attention.

"Excuse me, Ms. Maxwell."

"What?" Stunning blue eyes snapped in Isabel's direction. "Oh, it's you, Isabel."

"I'm sorry you're not getting the photos you want." Isabel whipped out her most winning smile. "I know all the best places on or around the property for you to take photos. Will you let me show you?"

The woman sniffed. "It's hopeless. A complete disaster. I knew I should've gone to Bahia Resort Hotel."

This was the exact sort of thing Isabel wanted to avoid. "I'm a huge fan. I've seen all your posts. I know the sort of places you love to go. Give me a chance."

"I don't know."

"And for your troubles, the hotel would love to offer you and your groom a post-wedding couple's massage tomorrow free of charge."

Isabel knew that Camilla had already enjoyed a ro-

mantic welcome basket as well as several complimen-
tary meals, but if the lifestyle blogger was happy, she
would rave about the hotel, and that was the best sort
of publicity.

"Fine," the blogger grumbled. "Show us where we
can get some halfway decent shots."

As soon as she made sure Camilla was happy with
the first location, Isabel headed inside to call the spa
and set up the massage appointment.

"… And make it free of charge. Thanks." Isabel hung
up the phone and jumped when a voice spoke behind
her.

"Do you make a habit of handing out free spa treatments?"

Isabel's pulse leaped as she glanced around and saw
Tom Busch standing behind her. His scowl told her he
wasn't happy.

"When I think it will benefit the hotel." She'd never
sucked up to the executive manager the way he preferred and often wondered if that had led him to shut
down her ideas for promoting The Opulence as a romantic destination.

"That's not your decision to make," Tom said. "You
should ask before comping anything."

"Usually I do." Isabel nodded, but continued to de-
fend her actions. "But today there wasn't time."

"We have procedures for how to do things here."

"I know, but I was trying to smooth over a situation
for Camilla Maxwell. She's a lifestyle blogger with almost four mill—"

Tom interrupted. "I don't care who it was for. Don't do it again."

"But—"

"Is there an issue here?"

To Isabel's dismay, Shane had approached while she and Tom had been speaking. Despite his neutral expression, she sensed he'd heard most if not all of the exchange. Being dressed down in front of him brought hot color to her cheeks.

"It's handled," Tom said, turning his back on Isabel in dismissal. "I wasn't expecting you today."

With the men engaged in conversation, Isabel snatched the opportunity to escape. Her blood continued to simmer as she headed toward the side terrace, where she'd left Camilla and her wedding party, but as she admired the picturesque tableau before her, her anger drained away.

The way Camilla and her groom stared at each other exemplified what Isabel worked so hard to achieve.

"Beautiful…" she breathed.

"Do you want to tell me what that was about?"

While she'd been absorbed in what was happening on the lawn, Shane had exited the building and come to stand beside her.

"I don't want to talk about it," she murmured. "Look how perfect this all is. This is what I've been talking about."

"Yes, it's quite nice." Shane might've been discussing a cup of coffee for all the interest he showed. "Why was Tom upset with you?"

"Because a crisis arose and I fixed it. Then I offered

Camilla and her soon-to-be-husband a free couple's massage for their trouble." Isabel glanced at Shane's profile, pausing a moment to appreciate his strong nose and bold eyebrows. She caught herself smiling and sighed. "See what's going on over there?"

"It looks like an ordinary wedding party to me."

"Far from ordinary. That's Camilla Maxwell. She is a huge lifestyle blogger on social media. I've followed her for years. She has the most amazing Instagram feed filled with fashion and travel photos. When she got engaged, I knew she could go anywhere to get married. So I reached out to her and pitched her on having her wedding at The Opulence. When those photos go up on her various online platforms, the hotel will get tons of publicity."

Isabel paused and turned to Shane. He glanced down at her, eyes narrowing as their gazes met.

"For the cost of a free spa treatment, The Opulence will be shown as one of the country's most beautiful spots to get married." She cocked her head. "Now tell me that's not worth breaking from procedure to accomplish."

Before Shane could answer, Isabel noticed that the photographer was done shooting this location. She started forward with a glance over her shoulder.

"Are you coming?"

"Coming where?"

"It's a surprise."

"I don't like surprises."

"Some surprises are very nice," she teased, walking backward a few steps so she could keep the conversation going. "You should open yourself up to the prospect of having fun."

Shane started following her. "Do I look like somebody who likes to have fun?"

"No," she admitted, resisting the urge to roll her eyes at him. "But you don't not look like someone who likes to have fun."

The ever-present line between his brows deepened. "What does that even mean?"

"It means you have potential."

After chewing on her comment for several seconds, he seemed disinclined to engage her flirtatious repartee. "Where are we going?"

"To a very picturesque spot so the bride and groom can take romantic pictures with Centennial Falls in the background. You're going to love how they'll look on the website."

Isabel introduced Shane to Camilla Maxwell before leading the way toward the path that ran along the top of the cliff to the falls overlook. Along the way, the photographer snapped the wedding party and the couple against the colorful fall foliage. The bride and groom in formal attire contrasted beautifully with the landscape. With each pause Camilla grew more satisfied with her wedding day photos so that by the time Isabel pitched her final destination, the blogger was eager to go.

"It's a little bit of a hike," Isabel warned. "But totally worth it."

Camilla's Instagram feed, filled with dramatic shots taken on her travels, demonstrated that the blogger was willing to take risks to get the wow shots.

"Lead the way."

They left the wedding party behind and headed down the trail to the bottom of the cliff and the lower viewing site for the falls. The abundant rains over the last few days had increased the river's volume and the falls were in their full glory. Isabel and Shane stood back while the photographer shot frame after frame of the couple with the falls and the resort in the background, muttering appreciative comments as he did so.

Afterward, Isabel escorted the couple to the golf cart she'd summoned to take them back to the resort.

"This was absolutely perfect," Camilla gushed, clinging to her groom's arm. "Exactly what I was hoping for when I booked my wedding here."

"I'm glad you're happy," Isabel said. "I can't wait to see the photos on your website and Instagram feed. And if you wouldn't mind, could the hotel use one or two for our website?"

"Of course."

Feeling victorious, Isabel smiled as she watched the couple go.

"That was nicely done," Shane said, breaking his silence for the first time in over an hour.

Isabel preened at his approval. "Thank you."

His gaze roved over her features, pausing at her lips, before shifting toward the trail. "I suppose we should be heading back."

She was enjoying this time with him too much to agree, but nodded because that was the sensible thing to do. Sensible? It struck her then that while she was trying to inject a little play into his work-focused mindset, he was having a transformative effect on her. Why be practical when what she really wanted to do was drag him to her favorite boulder in the center of the river and have a picture taken of them kissing with the falls as a backdrop?

As they started toward the trail, she snuck a peek at his somber profile and sighed. He was definitely not ready to venture from rock to rock across the river or to be photographed kissing her. Which of course led to her wondering if he'd ever kiss her again.

"So, your ex-girlfriend…" she began, bringing up the awkward situation instead of asking what she really wanted to know.

"What about her?"

"She booked her wedding at The Opulence next October."

"After the way you arranged the romantic proposal, I thought she might."

Warmed by his approving tone, Isabel continued, "I've already started researching the perfect theme for their special weekend. She loves to knit. Both she and Glenn like to run marathons and they have a darling golden retriever named Sunny."

Shane frowned. "How do you know all that?"

"I checked her out on social media."

He looked appalled. "You stalked her?"

"'Stalk' is such an aggressive term," she muttered. "I seek insight from social media cues. When someone contacts me about romantic things to do, or if a guy wants the perfect setting for a proposal."

"Like Glenn…"

"Exactly like Glenn." She beamed at him. "I will go to their Instagram feed or check out their Pinterest boards to see what sort of things they like. You can get a really good idea about people based on what they post online."

"I don't have any social media," Shane said.

"Yes." She nodded ruefully. "I'm well aware of that."

"You've looked?"

"I check out everyone I'm interested in." Her wry smile caused him to raise his eyebrows.

"I guess you're going to have to get to know me the old-fashioned way."

"Is that so," she purred. He was going to let her get to know him. That sounded promising. "I look forward to it."

They hiked in silence for nearly a minute before Shane spoke.

"So, what do you want to know?"

He continued to surprise her.

"Seriously? You'll answer my questions?"

"Possibly." He lifted one broad shoulder and let it fall. "I guess neither one of us will know what I'll answer until you ask."

Five

To Shane's surprise, Isabel didn't take him up on his offer to answer questions during their trek back to the hotel. Even more astonishing was his disappointment. As they drew within sight of the hotel, she paused and put her hand on his arm, stopping him. The touch sizzled through him, heightening his awareness of her soft lips and earnest hazel eyes.

"I want you to know how much I appreciate that you listened to me about my ideas for the hotel," she said. "I tend to lead with my emotions rather than logic. It's both a gift and a curse, and because of that, not everyone finds my ideas valuable."

"Of course." Recalling the scene he'd witnessed between her and Tom Busch earlier, Shane recognized that the executive manager wasn't interested in listening to such a junior employee. No matter how good her ideas might be. "And yet you've done a fine job presenting your ideas."

"In my career I've learned to be more organized." She wrinkled her nose. "It's my personal life where I tend to struggle with impulsive and chaotic urges."

"How so?"

"I love trying new things all the time. I can't tell you how many hobbies have caught my fancy only to end up dropped when something new and shiny catches my attention. I don't imagine you're like that at all."

"I don't have hobbies."

"Nothing? Not even golf or boating or gambling… what is it you do when you're not working?"

"I work out every morning. Running. Weights."

"Working out has 'work' in the title. I don't know if that qualifies it for a hobby. It's more like something you do to keep yourself healthy, like eating well. Unless training is something you feel passionate about."

What did he feel passionate about? His career. That wasn't exactly a hobby. And his drive to be successful was as much about thumbing his nose at his father as it was something that brought him deep satisfaction.

"I don't really have the time or energy to pursue interests beyond work."

"You can't plan to work this hard forever," she said. "Have you ever considered that you might benefit from some balance?"

Did she stop to think he might not appreciate her opinion on his personal life? Shane regarded her in silence for a long moment, before deciding she recognized that she'd overstepped and wasn't worried about it.

"What would you suggest?"

Her wry grin said it all. "I was done an hour ago."

"And you have something in mind that I might find interesting?"

"I might."

Shane didn't wait for her suggestion. "Do you want to have dinner?"

"Dinner?" Her hopeful expression sucker-punched him in the gut. "To discuss how today's photo shoot fits in with my ideas for the resort?"

Whether or not she'd meant to, Isabel had just handed him an out. He wasn't sure why he'd offered the invitation when he was determined not to cross a line with her again. But being with her was proving irresistible.

"We can definitely do that," he said, unable to express the conflicting emotions raging in him.

"That sounds great," she murmured, displaying sudden shy delight at his offer. "There's an Italian restaurant in North Bend that might be up to your standards." The town she mentioned was ten miles south of the hotel. "I need to go home and change. Would an hour from now be okay? I'll bring my laptop along and we can look at the photos from today's shoot. Jason said he'd upload everything right away and send me a link to his gallery."

"I'll see you in an hour."

Shane didn't follow Isabel when she headed into the hotel. Instead, he stood where she'd left him, massaging the back of his neck. What had he just done?

Stepped across the line, that's what. That she possessed a guileless idealism worried him. He'd seen too much. She hadn't seen enough. He had no business inviting her out for dinner.

Yet his instincts told him to stop fighting his interest in Isabel and take a chance for once. They might be as different as night and day, but the chemistry between them intensified with each encounter. He enjoyed her refreshing point of view and the fact that she challenged him to think of something besides his career.

An hour later, he'd exited his car in the parking lot of the Italian restaurant Isabel had suggested and was making his way to the front door when he noticed a bright orange Subaru BRZ wheeling off the highway. He paused to watch the sporty car execute a sharp turn into an open space. A moment later the driver's side door opened and a shapely leg emerged.

While Shane stared in mesmerized fascination, Isabel unfolded herself from the car, slung a tote bag over her shoulder and shut the door. Tonight she wore a snug cobalt dress that bared a great deal of thigh and paired it with a black leather moto jacket. Sexy and confident, she strolled across the pavement in his direction. Her high strappy heels gave her hips a natural roll that caused his heart to hammer. Aware he was gawking, Shane told himself to chill out, but the impact of her sassy smile on his libido couldn't be denied.

A strong urge to sink his fingers into her lush russet locks and bring her lips to his overrode his common sense. As she drew near, her perfume teased his senses. Maintaining a professional distance seemed less important by the second.

"You look great," he murmured.

"You sound surprised," she countered breathlessly, executing a slow pirouette so he could take her in from every angle. "I'm not as unsophisticated as my hotel uniform might suggest."

"I never thought anything like that."

"You did, but I forgive you." Her hazel eyes flashed. "And I'll admit that I dressed like this so you'd see a different side of me."

"You didn't need to." Shane took her arm and guided her toward the restaurant.

Isabel resisted. "What are you trying to say?"

"That I'm interested in you just the way you are."

"You're interested in me?" Her eyebrows climbed. She studied him for several steps. "How am I supposed to take that?"

"Why don't we go inside and find out over a glass of wine?"

But once the hostess settled them in a quiet booth and after ordering a bottle of Syrah from the local winery, the conversation veered toward that afternoon's photo shoot. Isabel slid onto the seat beside Shane and opened her laptop. While she scrolled through hundreds of photos, soliciting his opinion on several, he gave up trying to focus on her words and lost himself in her upbeat tone, her building excitement for the marketing potential and the zing of delight every time her shoulder bumped against his.

He wanted to nuzzle the spot where her dangly earrings bumped against her neck and slide his hand along her silky thigh. Her infectious grin invited him to relax and soak in all of her optimism and passion.

When the food came, she shifted to the opposite side of the booth and put away her computer. Shane immediately missed her proximity and wondered what spell she'd cast over him.

"How's the *costata di agnello*?" she asked, eyeing his rack of lamb with interest.

Shane realized he'd been so absorbed in watching Isabel savor every mouthful of her veal that he'd eaten a third of his dish without tasting a single bite. "Do you want to try it?"

"Please." She reached across the table and snagged a bit of the meat he'd cut. Eyes dancing, she popped the fork into her mouth and groaned. "Delicious."

After watching how much Isabel enjoyed the meal, Shane couldn't wait to see how she reacted to the decadent chocolate dessert the waiter suggested.

"You know, you're pretty young to be the head of a division the size of Richmond Hotel Group," Isabel said, spearing another bite of the flourless torte. "How long have you been with the company?"

"Five years." As he answered, Shane realized Isabel had been deftly interviewing him the entire meal while he knew next to nothing about her. "It's been a combination of hard work and luck."

"'I'm a great believer in luck, and I find the harder I work the more I have of it.' Thomas Jefferson," she said with a decisive nod. "So, where is all your hard work taking you next?"

"What makes you think I'm not perfectly happy with where I'm at?"

She gave that serious consideration for several seconds before asking, "Do you think you'll ever get to a point where you'll want more than what you have now?"

Like a wife and kids? He saw where her thoughts had taken her and decided to shut down that line of inquiry.

"What I have now is everything I need."

"What about sex?"

The blunt question left him choking on the sip of wine he'd just taken. Here he'd been thinking she was a local girl, naive and unworldly, and he the big bad sophisticate from the city. She kept turning the tables on him with her outrageous talk. Was she trying to get under his skin or did she just turn on the charm with everyone?

"What about it? I mean, I'm not a monk."

"So you date?"

"Of course," he said.

With a hint of mockery causing the corners of her lips to curve up, Isabel fixed him with bright curiosity. "How does the evening go?"

What did she want to know? Probably what any sensible woman on a date with a man hoped to hear. That he intended to get to know her before taking her to bed.

"I start with a nice dinner and…" He trailed off. Normally that's all he made time for.

"This is a nice dinner. Very romantic." She pointed to the half-eaten chocolate torte between them.

"You suggested the restaurant," Shane countered, registering his defensive tone.

She cocked her head and regarded him with a curious half-smile. "You let me eat off your plate and agreed to share a dessert."

He gazed at her baffled wonder. "So?"

"I'm surprised you let me, is all. It shows you're capable of intimacy."

"Intimacy?" He garbled out the word. "I was being polite."

He didn't do intimacy any more than he did romance. What was this woman doing? What was she thinking? Planning? As the questions sped up, his thoughts approached a state of near panic. And then he noticed she was smiling at him in absolute delight.

"When you take these women out that you date, what happens after dinner?" she asked, returning to her earlier line of questioning. "Dancing?"

"Like in a nightclub?" The thought of all that noise and the crush of so many people made him grimace. "No."

"A movie?"

He cleared his throat. "It's been a while since I've been to the theater." Years, in fact. Usually if he caught a popular film it was on TV, months after it left the theater.

"A romantic walk through the city?" Anticipating his dissent, she didn't even wait for him to respond. "So, after dinner you move straight to sex. Do you go back to her place or take her to yours?"

Shane shook his head, regretting that he hadn't stopped her flow of questions before this. A second later it occurred to him that she was looking for reassurance.

Despite the way she wore her romanticism like a suit of armor against all that was hard and unkind in the world, Isabel wasn't immune to disappointment or heartbreak. Today's encounter with Tom Busch was proof of that. She'd been visibly rattled by how the executive manager had dressed her down. Her earnest actions had been for the good of the resort and Tom's inflexibility had landed on her spirits like a ruler across the knuckles, painful and humiliating.

I'm not planning on seducing you, if that's what you're worried about.

That was what she deserved to hear. It was how he felt. He had no intention of taking advantage of her idealistic nature. But perversely this fact wasn't what came out of his mouth.

"It depends."

She popped a forkful of chocolate dessert into her mouth. "On what?"

"On whether I have any interest in seeing her again."

The invitation to attend a marketing meeting at the Richmond Hotel Group's offices in downtown Seattle arrived in Isabel's inbox the day after she and Shane had dinner at the Italian restaurant in North Bend. As he'd escorted her across the parking lot, Shane had made a passing comment about wanting her to present her ideas in person. She'd barely registered his remark because her blood had been rushing through her veins, making her deaf to everything but the music of longing and desire.

Would he kiss her again? Had the chocolate cake and

red wine been enough to purge garlic from her breath? Should she invite him back to her place? Would he expect her to? How far was she prepared to take things once she got him alone?

Only the first of these questions received an answer.

To her dismay, Shane had ushered her into her car and retreated with a polite smile, leaving her hormones revved up and her hopes dashed. She drove home, her confidence crushed beneath the weight of disappointment and doubt, and spent the rest of the night dissecting their dinner conversation.

Obviously the kiss on the bridge had been a fluke. A reaction to seeing his ex-girlfriend getting engaged and the manner in which Isabel had stirred him up with her talk of romance and the stage she'd set for a passion-filled encounter. He'd stepped right into her net and she'd been foolish enough to think that was the beginning of something.

In fact, it had been. Just not the something she'd hoped.

Yet, by the time Isabel entered the corporate offices of the Richmond Hotel Group, dressed in a chic black suit with skinny cropped pants and a silky white blouse, she'd shrugged off her initial regret and embraced the opportunity to show off her ideas. The meeting lasted two hours and went better than Isabel could've hoped. By the end, Isabel's best photographs and much of the copy from her original presentation to Shane had been approved for incorporation into the website and updated marketing materials. She was feeling giddy with success as she exited the conference room and shook hands with the marketing staff before making her way through the reception area.

"How did it go?"

Isabel had been so caught up in her thoughts, she didn't notice Shane had come up behind her and now stood with his hands in his pockets, staring at the elevator doors as they slid open. As he gestured for her to precede him, Isabel's heart began to hammer.

"It went great. They are going to make several changes to the website to include weekend romance packages as well as a page promoting the hotel as a romantic destination."

"Great." He pushed the button for the lobby and the doors slid shut. "I bet you feel like celebrating."

Mouth dry, she nodded. "I do."

Two days had passed since they'd had dinner. Two days when she'd obsessively checked her phone for some communication from him. Two days when she'd replayed every remark she'd made, every question and every answer. Had she said the right things? Was he interested? Maybe kissing her hadn't meant anything at all.

"Let's grab a drink."

"Sure." She stared at the descending numbers and tried to keep her expression casual while inside she was shrieking and dancing around like someone who'd won the lottery. "Where do you suggest? I don't know the area all that well."

"I know a spot."

She was certain he did. When they reached the curb, he ushered her into a waiting town car, and she watched downtown Seattle sweep past while her pulse throbbed so hard in her throat she couldn't speak, couldn't ask where they were going or tell him how much she appreciated the opportunity he'd given her.

Ten minutes later, the car stopped and they both slid out. Isabel gazed at the tall buildings around her. There wasn't a bar or even a restaurant in sight. Shane guided her through the doors into a residential building.

"Is this your place?" she croaked as they stood before a bank of elevators. She cursed her unsteady voice.

His eyebrow rose as he picked up on her nervousness. "Is that a problem?"

"Of course not." She wanted this. Wanted him. She didn't question if she was ready to take the next step with him.

Given the way their last evening had ended, the question remained if he was ready to take the next step with her. But surely she should be cheered by the fact that he'd invited her to his home.

"Relax," he murmured as the doors opened on the nineteenth floor. He set his fingers lightly against the small of her back and nudged her forward into the hallway. "We're here for a drink."

"I am relaxed."

One corner of his mouth gave a sardonic twitch as he punched in the key code that unlocked his door. "You look as skittish as a cat at a dog show."

With a single sound of disgust, she sailed past him and entered the unit. The first thing that struck her was the open space and the incredible view.

"Wow!" She set her purse on a table in the entry

and headed straight for the wall of windows. Her heels clicked on the polished limestone floors as she took in the view. Off to her left, the setting sun was bathing the skyscrapers in soft gold. "This is spectacular." Her gaze lingered on Mount Rainier. "And the views."

He came to stand beside her. "From the bedroom you can see Elliot Bay."

"I'd like that." She was only half teasing. Her heart raced, making it difficult to keep her tone light. "Lead the way."

"I'll give you a tour later."

Isabel didn't want a tour. She wanted him to take her to bed.

"The sun is setting," she countered, turning to face him. "It might be too late later."

Turning away from the view, he brought the full power of his dark brown eyes to bear on her. The anxiety that had risen in the elevator melted away as the chemistry between them began to bubble. After days of questioning how he felt about her, the penetrating questions in his somber gaze let her know he was interested.

So what was holding him back? She should ask, but for a change her fearless audacity failed her. This wasn't a situation where she took a man to bed for some casual fun. Since laying eyes on Shane a year ago, her heart and body had been laser-locked on him. Sex with him meant something to her. He meant something to her.

"I like that you left your hair down today," he said, the observation a thrilling peek behind the curtain that hid his thoughts. "It's such a beautiful color. And so soft."

"It's all natural," she said. "I'm all natural."

She had no idea what she meant by the remark, but he took the declaration in stride. His gaze drifted over her features before dipping lower. Isabel wished she'd worn something clingy and revealing instead of the silky blouse and suit jacket that only hinted at her curves.

"How did you get interested in hotel management?"

At the question, she barely stopped herself from rolling her eyes. Surely he hadn't brought her back to his place to ask about her career.

"I wanted to escape Washington and imagined myself living in some of the most exciting cities in the country. Instead, I ended up working for a hotel that isn't more than twenty miles from the small town where I grew up."

No doubt that sounded inexperienced to a sophisticated man of the world like Shane.

"Where did you get your degree?" he asked, strolling toward his big kitchen.

Isabel trailed after him and watched him open a bottle of champagne. He hadn't been kidding about celebrating.

"Washington State University's online hospitality program." She knew he'd graduated at the top of his class from Stanford and hoped he'd think her academic creds passed muster. "WSU is a top online program, and I really didn't have any way of attending school full-time because I needed to work to make ends meet. This way I was able to do all my classwork during my off hours."

After accepting a crystal flute from Shane, she

sipped champagne to cover her embarrassment at the way her defensiveness came through loud and clear. Usually she took pride in all she'd accomplished, but when she compared it to so many of the people around her, especially someone like Teresa St. Claire, what she'd done didn't seem all that impressive.

"It took me longer to finish," she continued, "but I graduated without having any school loans."

Even before Isabel's father had left them, there hadn't been a lot of extra money. Most of her clothes had come from thrift stores. Isabel's mother had brought home leftovers from her restaurant job. Anything to stretch a dime. Even now that she could afford it, Isabel lived without a lot of luxuries.

She remembered buying an expensive designer purse for her mother with her first paycheck from The Opulence and how her mother had been so shocked when she'd opened the beautiful box and peered beneath the delicate tissue paper. That her mother had been equal parts awed and appalled had taken some of the joy out of the purchase for Isabel. Right then and there she realized that her mother's thrifty ways had become such an intrinsic part of her that she couldn't begin to appreciate something she didn't absolutely need.

That made Isabel sad. She'd wanted to give everything to the woman who'd raised her and encouraged her. But it had also been a strong reminder that what was truly important was the love and support of those around her.

"And you've been with The Opulence for a year?" Shane asked.

"Yes."

"Any plans for where you'd like to go next?"

"New York, London, Paris, Italy or maybe somewhere in the Caribbean." She gave a breathless laugh. "I'm kidding. I know I don't have enough experience to get my dream hotel yet. And I like what I'm doing right now."

"Don't sell yourself short. I think you're destined for big things."

"I wasn't planning on selling myself short. I think I demonstrated to you that I have a pretty high opinion of myself."

"I have a high opinion of you, too."

Noticing that he hadn't poured a glass of champagne for himself, she set her glass down on the granite countertop. "I'd like a tour of your condo now. All of it. Starting with your bedroom."

Shane shook his head. "I didn't bring you up here for that."

"Then why did you?"

"I wanted to be alone with you." He regarded her through half-lidded eyes.

"Why? If you don't have any interest in sleeping with me."

Something flashed across his features. Something that turned her bones to oatmeal and heated her blood.

"Don't ever think I'm not interested," he growled, his gaze sweeping hungrily over her.

The sudden flare of sexual awareness tore through her, awakening a keen ache between her thighs. Desire pooled in her belly, the pressure a blissful discomfort.

"Then what's the problem?" she demanded, her voice liquid smoke.

"You work for me." With a blink he banked all the heat in his gaze, leaving her short of breath and lacking fulfillment of any kind. "I can't go there."

"Because that would break all sorts of rules." Stepping into his space, she slid her hand against his, rejoicing when he turned his palm to hers. A thousand goose bumps broke out on her skin as he played with her fingers. "And that's not who you are."

"It's all kinds of wrong," he murmured. Lifting his free hand, he drew his knuckles along her hot cheek. "You deserve more than I can give you."

That he hadn't shut her down yet gave her a glimpse into his soul. He could claim that work consumed his life, but he kept reaching out to her. She offered him something he couldn't bring himself to admit he needed. Fun. Passion. Fantasy.

"You know what your problem is?" she teased. "You're too tense."

The business suit he wore was a set of armor that insulated him from personal relationships. Isabel had no doubt that if she skimmed her hands up his chest and over his shoulders, sweeping the coat down his arms, he would loosen up. Hadn't he kissed her after witnessing Glenn's romantic proposal?

"What do you suggest?"

"We could polish off the bottle of champagne and follow that up with some shots. I'll bet it's been years since you've had too much to drink."

One dark eyebrow rose. "When you're around, I'm better off keeping my wits about me."

"You don't say." Hope flared at his admission. "Why is that?"

"Because you have a knack for making me do things I'll later regret."

"You do say the nicest things," she purred.

His body heat burned through his fine dress shirt as she stripped off his coat. She both heard and felt the sigh that expanded his chest. It was the sound of a man surrendering to the inevitable.

"There, now you look more comfortable," she said, tossing his coat onto a nearby chair and dropping her jacket beside it.

He stood with his hands on his hips, impassively watching her. Only the muscle bunching and relaxing in his jaw gave her any indication that he was at all affected.

"Your tie needs to go," she said, returning to him. She wrestled with his tie and it followed the path of his coat. "You'll feel much more relaxed when I'm done with you."

"I'm pretty sure where I'm headed is the opposite of relaxed," he muttered.

"You're just so buttoned up." Buttons slipped free beneath her shaking fingers. "You need to let loose."

As more and more skin came into view, Isabel found herself running out of ballsy moves. With more enthusiasm than finesse, she tugged his shirt free of his waistband and attacked the last three buttons. Knees weak with excitement, she parted the shirt and stepped back for a long ogle at his broad, muscular chest, making no attempt to conceal her awe.

"Damn." She gnawed her lower lip and looked him up and down, noting the bulge behind his zipper that said he approved of her decision to take his clothes off. "You're quite something."

He glared at her for several seconds while her heart pounded hard against her ribs. Isabel could see the conflict raging inside him. His nostrils flared as he drew in deep breaths. He gripped the edges of his shirt as if unsure whether to button it back up or tear it off. Tension vibrated in his muscles as he struggled with some internal demon.

"Oh, to hell with this," he growled.

Without warning, he bent down and set his shoulder into her midsection. The next thing Isabel knew, she was hanging upside down and staring at Shane's spectacular ass as he carried her out of the room.

Six

Cursing the string of bad ideas that had brought him to this point, Shane entered his bedroom and set Isabel on her feet beside the bed. Although she claimed she wanted to see the view from his bedroom, her gaze never strayed to the wall of windows where the sun was sinking toward the water.

He shouldn't be doing this. She worked for him. Telling himself that she wanted this as much as he did wasn't an excuse for stepping across the line. Maybe if it was pure lust he could've stopped, but something more than simple physical attraction called to him.

Losing himself in her soft hazel eyes, Shane lifted his hand and brushed his thumb over her lower lip. The edge of her bottom teeth was rough against the pad. Her long lashes drifted downward as he dipped his head and sucked her lower lip into his mouth. Stars exploded behind his eyes, lighting him up in a cacophony of sparks and longing and carnal lust.

Her palm skimmed over his bare chest and latched onto his biceps. She pushed up on her toes, asking for him to deepen the kiss, driving her mouth against his. He responded without hesitation. Holding nothing back. Pushing aside regrets. Reservations.

He slipped his tongue along hers and she met the thrust with raw hunger. He couldn't get enough of her mouth. The sweet taste of her. Eager. Open. Ravenous. He surrendered to the advance and retreat of lips and tongue, nearly losing his mind at the sexy sounds she made when she sucked his lower lip between her teeth and nipped him. The bite sharpened the lust clawing at him, but he tamped down his craving to take her hard and fast.

Recognizing doing decidedly naughty things with someone who worked for him was the height of stupidity, Shane couldn't stop himself from running his hands down her back and over her butt. Flexing his fingers into the soft curves, he lifted her against his growing erection. Her hands clung to his shoulders as he broke off the kiss to let his lips slide down her neck and into the hollow of her collarbone.

"We need to get naked," she declared, her fingertips tracing his abs, sending electrical charges along his nerves.

"We will."

Lifting her into his arms, he carried her the short distance to the bed. He lowered her onto the mattress and followed her down, settling beside her, one hand hooked over her hip, the other combing through her russet waves.

"I love your hair." He smiled down at her. "It feels like silk, and the color is warm and vibrant, just like you."

She blinked at him in blank bemusement for a second before poking him in the chest. "You've been hiding a poet in there."

"You bring that side out of me."

"Damn it, Shane Adams. That's the nicest thing you could've said to me." Her smile was like a sunset, warm and breathtaking as she curved her hand over his skull and pulled him down to her.

And then they were kissing again. Her tongue and teeth devouring him while he let her take the lead. Soon, however, he stole the control back and treated her to a kiss that left them both gasping and breathless.

"I am so turned on right now," she told him, spreading her legs wide so he could settle between them.

"Let's see if we can take that a notch or two higher."

"I'm ready when you are."

He hooked her thigh over his hip, rocking into her. She moaned, eyes closed, head thrown back, fingers busy with the buttons of her blouse. He watched her skin flush and her lips part. Her breathing grew erratic. Each sign of her mounting arousal fascinated him. Tracing her features with his gaze, he noted the placement of each freckle across her nose, the slight tilt to her eyes, the minor twist to her front tooth as it bit down on her plump lower lip.

Although his body ached to get her naked and come

inside her, he was content to savor this moment. Letting his passion build while watching hers rise to meet it was astonishingly satisfying. He had no desire to rush.

But then her shirt parted, revealing a lacy white bra and the upper curves of her breasts. A second later she'd popped the front catch, and his mouth went dry at the glorious sight of her fully exposed to him. Murmuring appreciatively, Shane dipped his head, nudged aside the white silk with his chin and slid his lips over her nipple, drawing it into his mouth.

The long, lusty cry that came pouring out of her caused his hips to buck, driving his erection against her. She arched her back, pushed her chest forward and pressed her soft flesh against his mouth. Alternating between sucking and lashing her with his tongue, he cupped his palm over her other breast and kneaded hard. She seemed to like it because she keened in pleasure. He circled his tongue around her tight nipple and grazed his teeth over the sensitive bud. Her head thrashed and she sank her fingers into his hair, nails digging into his scalp.

A flicker of sanity returned as her fingers eased past his belt, hunting for the part of him that was hot and hard. Groaning as her palm curved over his erection, he eased off her slightly so he could gaze down at her face. The determination in her eyes told him there was no stopping her. The breath he released was ragged and heavy with relief.

"Seriously," she panted, whipping off her shirt and bra before attacking his belt. "We need to get all our clothes off."

"If we do there's no going back."

"Are you trying to be noble?"

"I think I've already failed at that." He shut his eyes to block out her joyful, eager smile. "I need you to be sure you're okay with this."

"I'm completely okay."

He sighed and spoke the phrase that had crowded his thoughts since the first time they'd kissed. "I want you so much."

She kissed his neck and her lush hum tickled his skin, hardening him even more. "That's the best news I've heard in a year."

Returning the favor, he nuzzled her neck, opening his mouth on her sweet skin and sucking gently. "You smell like hot chocolate and pumpkin spice," he murmured, drawing the scent of her into his lungs.

"The idea was to make you want to devour me," she teased as he loosened the button on her pants and lowered the zipper.

Ever helpful, she lifted her hips off the bed so he could slide her pants and underwear off. He trailed his lips over her ribs and the flat plane of her belly, smiling at her sharp inhalation as he deposited kisses along her thighs, then stripped off her shoes and pants, baring her to his gaze.

"Beautiful," he murmured, sliding his palms over her warm, soft flesh, savoring the view of her pale skin. "Absolutely gorgeous."

She shifted onto her knees and avoided his gaze as she reached for his zipper. As she tugged down his pants, he realized his compliments appeared to have had the opposite effect from what he'd intended. Instead of basking in his admiration, she suddenly looked uncomfortable.

"What's wrong?" he asked, sliding off the bed so he could step out of his shoes and pants. He set his fingers beneath her chin and tipped her head until she met his gaze.

"You called me beautiful," she admitted. "I'm just not used to it."

"But you should be." And then he started to understand. "You lavish so much energy on other people's perfect moments that you neglect to create some of your own."

"I guess that's true." Her eyes narrowed as her sparkle returned. "And remarkably insightful."

"Let me make your fantasies come true."

"Oh," she moaned, a truly beautiful noise that made him grin. "That would be nice."

Shane dropped his boxer briefs to the floor and located a condom in his nightstand. After rolling it on, he moved onto the bed and gathered Isabel into his arms. Their eyes met, and Shane glimpsed endless vulnerability and longing in those hazel depths. She was giving him everything and taking a huge risk in the process. Humbled and filled with awe, he kissed her with as much tenderness as his raging body could manage.

She wrapped one arm around his neck and set her palm against his cheek as he slid his hands down her body. Trembling, she opened herself to him, her breath growing shallow and uneven beside his ear as he dipped his finger into her heat. A shudder ripped through her, and he loved that she was so turned on.

"I need you now," she pleaded, tugging his hip and spreading her thighs wider so that he fell into the sexy cradle between them.

Nearly insane with lust, he shifted until he could rub the tip of his erection against her sweet, slippery core. She moaned his name as he pushed forward. Shane hissed out a breath as he entered her in one smooth stroke.

"Wow," he declared, the word ripped from him because she felt so damned good.

"Oh, yes." Her eyes were closed, lips parted, a woman lost in desire. "And more."

Already a snug, wet fit around him, she clenched down even harder as he drew out and filled her once more. Now it was Shane's turn to moan as her cries drove his lust higher. He rocked into her over and over, starting slow, finding a rhythm and pace that she liked. She matched his every thrust, grinding against him, her motions growing bolder and more wild as her own pleasure climbed. And he loved watching her.

Suddenly her eyes snapped open and she smiled when she caught him watching her. "I can handle all you've got," she purred, her voice all sexy smoke and raw vulnerability.

"You sure?" He pushed deeper, stopped and gauged her reaction in the flaring of her eyes and the upward curve to her lips.

She hooked her legs around his back, pulling him tighter, and brought her lips to his ear. "Oh, yes."

So he answered her call, burying himself inside her, thrusting hard until she screamed his name with such fierce determination that he knew she was right on the edge. She rocked into him, finding the perfect friction, and let her pleasure rip. The orgasm blasted through her. She shuddered and shuddered again, squeezing her eyes shut to hold on to it as long as possible.

"I'm coming." Her hoarse shout unleashed his own climax.

The damn thing had snuck up on him as he'd watched Isabel come undone and ripped into Shane with the shock of a lightning bolt. His skin tingled. Pleasure so acute it was painful rolled through him. Shuddering in the midst of his own orgasm, Shane had to bite his lip to keep back the words that wanted to flow out of him.

On the verge of a dangerous confession, he rode the waves of pleasure with his teeth clamped together. As he collapsed onto the mattress beside Isabel, he reached a place of reckoning. Never before had he known a moment like the one he'd just shared with Isabel. It wasn't just great or even fantastic sex. With her, he'd been moved to a whole new level of intimacy and ecstasy.

It terrified him that it had never been that good before.

Because he already knew he wanted more. And more could lead to a situation neither one of them was prepared for.

With four days remaining until the guests would start arriving for the Richmond retreat, Teresa had several items to go over with the hotel's event planner, Aspen

Wright. She'd made no secret of resenting that Teresa was calling the shots. No doubt Aspen saw this as management's doubting of her ability. Whatever the case, she was making Teresa's life hell.

"This isn't the setup we discussed," Aspen said, hurtling yet another protest at Teresa.

"Yes, it is," Teresa responded, forcing a smile onto her tight lips. "I said early on that the room will work better for Jessie Humphrey's performance set up with eight rounds."

"The problem is that I'm not sure I have enough tables here at the moment, and with the storm, it's really hard to get deliveries."

Teresa stuck to her guns. "This needs to be done." Her seating chart depended on it.

Although Aspen probably thought she was being unreasonable, the smaller tables of eight offered more intimacy among the party guests.

"Also, I don't know I can if I can do a quick enough turnaround with the linens. At the moment we only have half of what you need."

"You knew what I was requesting," Teresa said. "Why don't you have them?"

"We had a wedding this weekend. Our linen service is delayed because of the storm."

Teresa wanted to shriek. "See what you can do. If we need to change to white linens instead of the ivory then I need to know."

It seemed like a small distinction, but everything needed to be perfect.

"Where are we at with the gold chargers?" Teresa asked, holding her breath.

"We have enough," Aspen said. "But I'll need to see if I have enough mirrors for the centerpieces now that you've changed the number of tables."

I didn't change the number of tables.

"Get it done."

Teresa headed back toward the lobby in a snappish mood that became even more vile as she observed the body language of the couple walking toward the concierge desk. Weeks earlier she'd noticed that Isabel Withers had the hots for the handsome president of Richmond Hotel Group, but figured between Shane's tunnel vision when it came to work and Isabel's vibrant personality, the two would mix like toothpaste and orange juice.

She'd been dead wrong.

To Teresa's surprise, not only was the oh-so-serious Shane Adams showing off his even white teeth in a fond grin while Isabel prattled and gestured, he was behaving even more out of character by ignoring the smartphone ringing in his hand so he could focus on her one hundred percent.

Teresa didn't get it. What was it about Isabel that had transformed Shane into a personable human being? Granted, the woman was pretty, but not really a standout in her severe navy hotel uniform, her russet hair swept into a sleek French twist. Yet this didn't seem to bother Shane in the least. He appeared captivated by Isabel's gregarious smile and playful banter. Her passionate nature had struck the right note with the stoic pragmatist.

Obviously something had transpired between Isabel and Shane. Was it possible that the workaholic had been influenced by the romantic atmosphere of The Opulence and had succumbed to the concierge's abundant charms? If so, it was definitely a demonstration of opposites attracting. From what Teresa had gleaned about the hotel employee and executive, the only trait they shared was that they were both massively organized individuals.

Envy swept through Teresa like an ill wind.

The unfairness of her own failed romance with Liam made her want to stamp her feet and whine like a child denied its favorite candy. Instead, she did something so much worse.

When Shane stepped away to take his call, Teresa approached Isabel.

"I wouldn't go there if I were you," she warned.

"Go where?" Still wearing a smitten half grin, Isabel tore her attention from Shane's retreating figure and looked at Teresa.

"You and Shane. That's a recipe for disaster."

Eyebrows climbing, Isabel asked, "Why would you say that?"

"Because you two aren't the least bit compatible." Teresa recognized that the sorry state of her own love life was not a good reason to give romantic advice to someone who hadn't asked for her opinion.

"We're opposing forces that make up a dynamic whole," Isabel countered lightly, her expression showing more empathy than annoyance.

Teresa exhaled impatiently. Not long ago she'd been

over-the-moon happy with Liam. But at the first little hiccup, he'd turned on her. Okay, maybe the huge gift his father had settled on her was more than a little hiccup, but instead of getting to the heart of Linus's motivation, Liam had accused her of lying to him about their relationship.

"What I know," Teresa began, "is that attraction and sex—even great sex—aren't enough to make a relationship work."

"Of course." Isabel agreed amicably. "But chemistry is a good enough place to start. And if you find somebody who you can believe in, someone who every time they smile it gives you butterflies, who makes you feel better just from being with them—isn't it worth the risk?"

Teresa thought about the hundreds of butterflies that had taken flight on the dance floor the first time she and Liam had kissed and the hot rush of passion that had them tearing off each other's clothes that night in her office. The way her heart had stopped when he'd invited her to stay with him during the Richmond retreat and how it had then raced as she realized what a big step it had been for him to ask.

"I don't think that any romance is worth the risk," she grumbled, all too aware that this was not the same song she'd been singing two short weeks ago.

"I guess that's where you and I differ," Isabel said. "If I don't take a risk and open my heart, then I might never be truly happy."

Teresa reeled in her skepticism, reminding herself that Isabel touted herself as a romance concierge. Part of her ability to charm couples was that she threw herself heart and soul into the fairy tale of true love and romance.

"I get goose bumps whenever he comes near me. I wish I could bottle the feeling and sell it in the gift shop." Her engaging grin was like a sunrise, filling Teresa with all things hopeful and optimistic. "I'm tired of being alone," Isabel continued. "I want to have a partner. Have someone to share my success with. I've worked hard this last year and put all my energy into my job. You know what I found out? Success isn't satisfying with no one to share it with."

Isabel's words struck to the heart of what Teresa had realized in the last month. Those moments when she and Liam had started to mesh had made her problems easier to handle and her victories so much sweeter. Unfortunately, it also meant that the crash, when it came, was so much more painful. She wanted to spare Isabel that hurt.

"I can tell you Shane Adams isn't that person."

"You don't know that," Isabel protested.

"I do know it because he's like me. Work consumes him." Teresa took no pleasure in delivering these cold, hard facts, but Isabel needed a reality check. "His career is everything. You're delusional if you think he's going to stop working long hours and make time for you. You deserve someone who's going to get all mushy and romantic. He's not that guy."

"I disagree," Isabel countered, sounding defensive for the first time. "He has promise."

"And don't forget you work for him," Teresa persisted, throwing out more obstacles for Isabel to consider. "He's not going to cross that line."

"What if he did?"

The hint of pink beneath Isabel's fair skin betrayed her. Teresa glanced from the concierge to the tall executive and tried to ignore the stab of envy when she noticed the way Shane's dark gaze lingered on Isabel.

"Look, whatever's going on between you two, the reality is that Richmond Hotel Group is his top priority, and he will always choose to do what benefits the company and his career over what's best for you."

"You might be surprised."

Although they were close to the same age, at this moment Teresa felt world-weary and far too experienced. "For your sake, I hope so."

Seven

Clouds hung low over Tiger Mountain, obscuring the top as Liam drove east along I-90. He kept glancing at them as he ticked off the miles until his exit. These weren't the wispy cirrus or fluffy white cumulus variety that floated serenely across the blue sky, but ominous blankets of nimbus gray that warned of impending storms. Liam felt their oppressive threat like a solid weight on his mood as he pondered what sort of hell the next week would have in store for him.

With the upcoming Richmond retreat set to start in four days, he hadn't expected to be heading up to The Opulence this soon, but with Matt Richmond off the grid with the woman he loved, Liam felt honored to be trusted with the final preparations. The event was important to Matt, and Liam wasn't going to let his best friend down. That this meant he would come into contact with Teresa constantly, Liam was trying to put out of his mind.

He was a professional. He could act like one. Plus, these encounters would let him practice detachment for the next board meeting when he'd have to introduce her as their newest member while keeping his antipathy concealed.

Days earlier he'd visited his lawyer and discovered that contesting the will could make the matter drag on for years and years. Liam had decided the quickest and most efficient way of handling the situation was to have the lawyer draft a document where Teresa would agree to sell him shares at the end of her stint on the board. He intended to present it for her to sign before the end of the retreat.

With the wipers clearing mist from his windshield in an intermittent beat, Liam exited the freeway and began winding his way along the two-lane road twisting through the tree-lined foothills. Despite the tranquil views offered at each new turn, his agitation grew as the distance to the hotel diminished.

Deny though he tried, his emotions were stirred up at the thought of seeing Teresa again. As much as he wished logic and suspicion had dumped ice water over his passion for her, his body and mind remained at odds. Unlike so many women he'd dated in the past, Teresa had burrowed under his skin and was proving difficult to dislodge.

As Liam turned the car into the hotel's driveway, he realized he was grinding his teeth and made a de-

termined effort to relax his jaw before stopping at the
lobby entrance. After handing off the car to a waiting
valet, he stepped across the threshold, bellhop and luggage in his wake, and briefly paused to gaze about The
Opulence's enormous lobby.

He didn't realize he was searching for Teresa until
he noticed his disappointment. Much to his dismay, lo-
cating her in a room had become second nature to him.
The woman had gotten past his guard to such an extent
that he thought about her constantly. The memory of
her delicate scent clung to his mind like cobwebs. That
night on the dance floor when they'd kissed for the first
time. The hot, fast coupling on the couch in her office.
The slower, leisurely exploration that happened later
that night.

He craved the warmth of her fingers against his skin.
The taste of her sweet lips. The sexy sounds she made
as she climaxed.

His body stirred, betraying him. Damn it. He had to
stop thinking about her like that.

Narrowing his focus, he caught the eye of an attractive redhead at the concierge desk and headed toward her.

Her hazel eyes glinted, indicating recognition. "Hello,
Mr. Christopher. Welcome back to The Opulence."

"Hello, Isabel," he said, reading the name tag fas-
tened to her uniform. "Can you take care of checking
me in and getting my luggage to my suite?"

"Of course." Isabel typed away on her computer for
a few seconds. "Let's see what we have scheduled for

you. Looks like you have a dinner reservation at the Overlook tonight at eight."

"That'll work," he said, thinking that would give him time to get an update on the retreat preparations from Teresa and catch up on some work emails. He glanced around the lobby, noting several attractive women eager to make eye contact. Their interest made him smile. It was time he put himself back on the market, and any of them would be a delightful companion. He would grab a drink in the bar later and invite one to dinner.

"And a private dinner for two scheduled for your suite the day after tomorrow at eight."

A private, romantic dinner he and Teresa would've shared. Liam's heart gave an ungainly lurch as he crashed back into the conversation. Before finding out his father had left Teresa shares in Christopher Corporation, he'd been planning to spend at least part of the retreat romancing Teresa.

"You can cancel the dinner in my suite," he said shortly. "My plans have changed. If you could book me a table for two at the Overlook tomorrow at seven instead." He had already confirmed that Shane Adams was free.

Isabel nodded and typed away. "Also, just to confirm that you have a reservation at the spa scheduled Wednesday evening at six."

Apparently his assistant had been quite thorough in orchestrating a romance-filled stay.

"You can cancel all the spa treatments," he told her in a clipped tone. "I'm here to work."

"Of course, but you really shouldn't miss the Turkish Hammam Rub and Scrub followed by our Desert Sage

Massage. It's quite a treat. I'm sure you know many of our guests come to stay with us specifically because of the excellence of our spa."

"I really don't need a scrub or a massage," he said, ignoring the way his shoulder muscles protested otherwise.

"Are you sure?" Isabel coaxed, her smile encouraging. "Everyone can use a little pampering now and then."

Liam recalled Matt raving about the quality of the spa here. Although it wasn't usually his thing, maybe a massage would help him relax before the big event. "Fine," he grumbled. "I'll keep the spa appointment."

"Wonderful." Isabel's infectious grin seemed to indicate he'd made the right decision. "Is there anything else I can do for you?"

"I don't suppose you know where Teresa St. Claire might be at the moment."

"I believe Teresa is checking on a delivery for the Richmond retreat. The weather has caused some delays in shipments. How did you find the roads between here and Seattle?"

"Fine." But had they been? Liam cursed silently, realizing he had no idea. He'd been too preoccupied with his thoughts to notice his surroundings. "Manageable," he amended, feeling foolish.

"That's good. We have a lot of people arriving here over the next few days, and with all the rain we've had, it wouldn't surprise me if a mudslide blocked the highway."

"Let's hope not."

"Do you want me to let Teresa know you're here?"

Did he? Or had he jumped in his car and driven to the hotel in hopes of ambushing her?

Gripped by an urge to do just that, Liam turned down the concierge's offer. He had no prepared contract to deliver to Teresa. So what was he doing here? He could be overseeing everything for Matt from his office in Seattle. Why the overwhelming urge to see her again?

The answer came to him abruptly. He wanted answers. He needed her to convince him all the assumptions he was making were wrong. Beneath this simple explanation, however, lingered a far more complicated motive. Despite his anger with her, his suspicions about what she'd done to convince his father to give her part of the family business, Liam wanted to be near her. To lose himself in her.

"I'm sure she'll be glad to see you," the pretty concierge continued.

On that point they disagreed. "I'm going to grab a drink and check in with my office. If she comes by, send her toward the bar."

Despite being convinced that it was a bad idea to mix alcohol, his volatile emotional state and seeing Teresa again, Liam headed into the bar and settled into a corner with a manhattan and his smartphone. At some point on the drive from Seattle, Matt had sent a text with an attached photo of a romantic shot of him dipping his new bride in a passionate kiss.

She said I Do!

The gorgeous tropical beach. The couple looking so damned happy. Liam stared at the photo for a long time before forcing his fingers to type the obligatory congratulations. Not that Liam begrudged Matt his happiness. Nadia was perfect for him and that they'd found each other was fantastic.

Liam recognized that if his relationship with Teresa had worked out, he might've felt more like celebrating his friend's good fortune. Instead, he was left to grumble that fate wasn't always kind and to wonder if maybe he wasn't cut out for love.

An hour later, he was wrapping up a call to the head of his marketing department when he spotted Teresa crossing the lobby. Classically elegant in a cream pencil skirt and black blouse with a slim gold watch and small hoop earrings, she looked captivating. No plunging necklines, leg-baring hemlines or flamboyant accessories for her. Just consummate professionalism. No one would ever suspect she became an alluring temptress in private.

His heartbeat surged as he watched her pause near the giant flower arrangement at the center space, glaring at the display as if it offended her. It took him a second to realize she wasn't upset with the flowers, but the person she was speaking to on the phone.

Abandoning his second manhattan, Liam headed her way, ignoring the way his nerves jangled in anticipation of being near her again. As he drew within earshot, he noticed her staring at her phone screen as she swore under her breath.

"Something wrong?" Liam asked, pricked by satisfaction when she whirled to face him.

Was it his imagination, or for an instant had she looked pleased to see him? No doubt she believed he'd come here to apologize. If so, that demonstrated just how little she knew him.

"Jessie Humphrey is supposed to be flying in from New York for the party," she explained, "but she's nervous about the weather and I'm not sure if she's going to come. Matt is going to freak if I can't produce a headliner for Saturday night." For a moment her frown deepened, and then, as if realizing what she'd revealed, she shifted topics. "What are you doing here?"

"Matt is on his honeymoon and asked me to keep an eye on things until he gets back."

"Matt and Nadia got married?" She looked shocked and happy and sad all at once. "Wow, that was fast."

"That was my reaction, too," Liam murmured as their gazes came together and locked for the space of a breath. In that moment it was as if they shared a single thought.

That could've been us...

"Well, good for them," Teresa said, shifting her gaze away. Her phone rang and she glanced at the screen. "I have to take this." And without waiting for him to respond, she answered the call. Even before she started to speak, she'd begun shifting her feet in a slow side pass that put space between them. "Hey, Jeannie, thanks for calling me back. Really, the weather isn't that bad here." She gave an awkward little laugh. "It's Seattle. We have rain all the time." A pause while she listened. As she continued to put distance between them, Teresa rubbed her shoulder as if easing an ache. "Please, if you'll reassure her..."

Liam waited until Teresa disappeared down a hallway before pulling out his phone. With his body and mind at war, he dialed a number, all the while telling himself he was acting for Matt's benefit and not because he wanted to help Teresa.

"I have something I need you to do," he told the person who answered. "Jessie Humphrey is supposed to be performing at an event near Seattle, but she's worried about traveling because of the weather. My assistant, Duncan, can get you the details. I need you to make certain she gets here on time."

"I see your honey is back."

"Really?" Isabel's gaze shot up from the computer screen and raced around the lobby. Her heart and loins pulsed in time, sending her blood pressure skyrocketing.

In the days since she'd spent the night with Shane in Seattle, she'd heard from him once by text, a straightforward response to her announcement that she'd made it back to Centennial Falls in one piece.

Glad you arrived safely. I enjoyed our time together.

Five simple words to fuel her daydreams and spawn a wide variety of fantasies about what would happen when she saw him again.

"Relax," Aspen said, her tone amused. "He's meeting with Teresa to go over the menu for the retreat's opening night cocktail party." The event coordinator shook her head. "Girl, you've got it bad."

Noting the throb between her thighs as she recalled

Shane's hands and mouth gliding over her skin, Isabel agreed. "What can I say? The heart wants what the heart wants."

Aspen made a derogatory noise. "Your heart is going to end up flattened like a pancake if you aren't careful. That man isn't going to come within fifty feet of you."

Isabel bit the inside of her lower lip to avoid spilling to her best friend that he already had. In fact, he'd come within her three times. An irresistible smile formed on her lips.

"I appreciate your wisdom," Isabel said, "but you might be underestimating my charm."

"I'm not. You are intelligent and adorable. Any smart single man would snap you up in a second."

"How can you say he's not smart?" Isabel shot her friend a coy smile. "He graduated top of his class from Stanford."

"There's book smarts and then there's street smarts." Aspen sobered. "That man wouldn't recognize a prize like you if you were naked and pole dancing for him."

Aspen's vivid imagery sent a spear of lust straight through Isabel. "He might…"

"He's all business. You don't have a chance." Aspen squeezed Isabel's arm. "I just don't want to see you get hurt."

"I know."

Aspen's arguments echoed Teresa's advice, but Isabel didn't want to focus on the consequences of getting involved with Shane Adams. Being with him was like visiting an amusement park, all thrill rides and sugary treats. She knew it wouldn't last, but the experience would make her smile for a long time.

"I'd better get back to work." Aspen sighed. "The Richmond retreat isn't going to set itself up."

Distracted by an email that had popped into her inbox, Isabel said goodbye to her friend and opened the message. It was from Tom Busch, the executive manager. He wanted to see her in his office in an hour. The request was unusual. Tom preferred to deal with the top rungs in his management structure. Isabel reported to the front office manager, who in turn reported to the executive manager.

She thought about the confrontation she'd had with Tom when she'd comped Camilla Maxwell's couple's massage and wondered if this was her moment of reckoning.

"Isabel, come on in."

Fighting down a mixture of nerves and annoyance, Isabel pasted on a pleasant smile and perched on one of Tom's guest chairs. He ignored her for several seconds while he regarded his computer screen. Isabel guessed the move was supposed to increase her discomfort. It worked.

At last Tom turned his gaze on her. "How are the preparations going for the guests who will be attending the Richmond retreat?"

She relaxed minutely at the mundane question. "Most everyone attending has responded and we've booked everything they've requested." As she spoke, Tom was nodding his head, not really listening to her answer.

"We're prepared to handle anything that comes up at the last minute."

"You're probably wondering why I brought you up here."

Her stomach tightened. "Yes."

"Several weeks ago you came to me with an idea for marketing the hotel as a romantic destination. I've given it some thought and decided that it's a good idea."

Wait...what?

He'd decided it was a good idea?

If he'd brought this up before she'd pitched the idea to Shane, she might feel a rush of satisfaction. But after Shane had arranged for her to meet with corporate marketing, putting his stamp of approval on the romantic destination concept, to hear Tom take credit for what Shane had already decided tied her stomach into knots. Nor could she confront the executive manager about the lie without exposing her personal connection to Shane.

Isabel's cheeks burned as she said, "That's great. I've been working on some ideas—"

"Yes, yes, of course. But I'm really interested in this whole concept of a romance concierge." Tom was smiling now, but he looked through her as if she was a piece of furniture. "I found someone who fits the bill perfectly."

Isabel couldn't believe what she was hearing. It was her idea. She was the romance concierge. Why was he bringing in someone else to do what she was perfectly suited for?

"What?" she demanded, barely able to breathe. "Who?"

"I hired a lifestyle blogger with several million followers. Camilla Maxwell. Apparently she had her wedding here last weekend. Do you know her?"

Did Isabel know her?

"I was the one who reached out to her and suggested she get married at The Opulence." Even as she tooted her own horn, Isabel could see Tom wasn't listening. The unfairness of it all turned Isabel's voice to sandpaper. "But she's a blogger and doesn't know anything about the hotel industry. Why did you choose her?"

"She's featuring her wedding at The Opulence on her blog as well as social media and promoting the hotel as an ideal romance destination. She'll be perfect."

As she listened to Tom, Isabel realized that the executive manager hadn't come to the decision on his own. He'd been told about the change in marketing direction by Shane. "Corporate agrees this concept is a wonderful idea. An influencer like Camilla would bring greater awareness to the hotel."

"I don't understand how it will work," Isabel protested. "Is she moving here?"

"Oh no. She'll be the face of the program. She's a stunning woman, after all. People will believe they're contacting her for their personalized romantic experience." He paused for a beat. "Of course we'll need you to handle all the arrangements."

After she'd poured her heart and soul into the project, someone else was going to swoop in and take credit for it? Worse, Isabel was going to have to do all the grunt work? Outrageous. Nor would she quit. Isabel loved what she was doing. It suited her. But to have her hard work go unrecognized?

"I thought," Isabel murmured, a lump in her throat making her voice sound tinny and raw. "The romance concierge would be my role."

Tom wasn't interested in playing fair when he could take credit for her ideas. "No," he corrected her. "You're the hotel's *concierge.*"

Crushing disappointment made her eyes fill with helpless tears. She stared at her clasped hands and struggled for composure. How could Shane have done this to her?

Corporate agrees.

Suddenly, Teresa's words came back to haunt Isabel. Shane would always choose what was best for the hotel over what was good for her. The betrayal cut deep, shaking her confidence in the connection she thought she had with Shane. So much for believing she was the master of all things romantic. He'd warned her that he wasn't interested in such things. His time with her had been about scratching a sexual itch.

"That's all I have for you," Tom said. "You can go back to your post."

Drowning in humiliation, she fled Tom's office. While she understood from a marketing standpoint why Shane would lean toward an influencer like Camilla Maxwell, she couldn't believe he would do that to her. Almost as devastating was that he'd had Tom break the news...

Before Isabel reached the lobby, she slipped into a

quiet alcove and fought to get her emotions back under control. Seesawing between anger and despair, she texted Aspen.

Do you have time for a drink after work?

Aspen's answer came immediately.

Always. Where?

Isabel suggested their usual haunt in town. The rustic bar and grill was a far cry from The Opulence's luxurious ambiance and exquisite cuisine and the perfect place to complain about their boss. Drained by her heightened emotions all afternoon, Isabel entered the bar and found her friend sitting in a booth by the front window. When she slid into the bench opposite, Aspen looked her over and grimaced.

"What happened?"

Isabel signaled their usual waitress and ordered a dirty martini. "Tom decided to pursue my idea to promote The Opulence as a romantic destination."

"That's great." Aspen noted Isabel's stormy expression and backpedaled. "Or not great. What happened?"

"He shut me out. He hired Camilla Maxwell as the face of The Opulence's romance concierge. Only I get to do all the work."

"And not get any of the credit." Aspen hissed out a breath. "Why would he do that? It was your idea and you're the perfect person to do it. Hell, you've been doing it for the last eight months."

"Tom made it seem like it was his idea, but he had no interest in the whole romance destination idea when I pitched it before." Although now that she thought about it, once Shane brought the idea up, Isabel could see Tom tripping over himself to impress the boss.

"Well, that's not a surprise. The man hasn't had an original idea since he came to the hotel."

"But what if Shane is the one who suggested hiring Camilla because he doesn't think I'm good enough?"

He'd never given her any indication that's what he thought, but how well did she know him, after all? Plus, Teresa and Aspen had reminded her that as an executive, Shane's top priority was the company. And what if Shane thought she'd slept with him to curry favor? Would that make him overlook her for advancement?

"I'm sure he doesn't think that." Aspen gave her a sympathetic head tilt. "He just wants what's best for the hotel. And most of the time executive types like Shane don't even notice the little people like us."

"Shane noticed me," Isabel said, resenting her friend's doubting expression. "He *likes* me."

Aspen's expression went from puzzlement to astonishment in a heartbeat. "Please tell me nothing happened between you two."

"We have a connection." Seeing that she wasn't convincing Aspen, Isabel grew defensive. "I know what you're thinking. I had no business getting involved with Shane."

"Actually, that's not what I was thinking at all." Aspen shook her head sadly.

"Okay," Isabel said. "Maybe that's what I've been

saying to myself since meeting with Shane. I thought he was different. I thought I meant something to him."

"Are you going to ask him about it?"

"What if he tells me I wasn't good enough?" Her chest tightened as she was pummeled by a double dose of self-doubt and shame.

Aspen reached across the table and squeezed Isabel's hand. "You're good enough."

"You're my friend so of course you'd say that, but right at this moment I don't feel like I'm ever going to amount to anything."

The urge to drop her head onto her arms and start crying overwhelmed Isabel. She bit the inside of her lip until she'd mastered her emotions.

"So, what are you going to do?"

"I'm tempted to quit." Her spirits plummeted at the thought of leaving the Richmond Hotel Group. She really liked the company and until Tom Busch had become the executive manager, she believed she was making a difference.

"As much as I'd miss you, I've said for a long time that your talents are wasted here. You have all the skills you need to move past a job as a concierge."

"That's exactly what I needed to hear."

She hadn't expected that in the end none of her hard work, innovation or customer service skills would get her noticed. Often her friends had warned her that she was a shade too optimistic, but Isabel had never let adversity slow her down before. So why now? Because what had happened between her and Shane had been personal and remarkable. Or maybe she'd been kidding herself all along.

"You're meant to do bigger things," Aspen told her. "So update your resume and find a job working for someone who will appreciate you."

Images of her time spent with Shane bombarded her, making her heart ache. "I thought I already had."

Eight

After retreating to her hotel suite to kick off her shoes and order a late lunch from room service, Teresa gave herself half an hour to doze in the comfortable armchair. The combination of insomnia, long work days and the cozy warmth of the fireplace's hypnotic flame made her eyelids heavy, and she saw no reason to resist the lure of a twenty-minute nap. Unfortunately, before she fully nodded off, her phone vibrated against the dresser's hard surface, jolting her back to wakefulness.

As the days until the Richmond retreat counted down, Teresa was starting to dread every time her phone buzzed. This happened a lot. On average, at least five things went wrong each hour that required her input.

Although she'd done events for the ultra-wealthy before, nothing had been on quite this scale. Before when she dealt with this level of A-listers, she'd arranged a single event or something over the course of the day. This was a three-day extravaganza, wining and dining and entertaining the sort of people who were used to the finest of everything.

The phone buzzed again, rousing Teresa from her thoughts. This time the call was from Isabel.

"Hey," she said. "What's up?"

"There's a reporter here, looking for you," Isabel said.

Panic flared through Teresa at the news. Had the man who'd threatened her several weeks ago tipped off a reporter about the things Joshua had been up to and the lengths Teresa had gone to hide her brother's illegal activities? Or had Joshua himself let something slip? As much as Teresa loved her brother, she knew he hadn't demonstrated his ability to make good decisions.

"Did they give you a name?" Teresa asked, telling her pounding heart to slow down. The Fixer had done his work and erased all trace of Joshua's bad behavior. If this was a smear campaign there wouldn't be much by way of proof. Or so she hoped.

"She didn't have to," Isabel confided, the smile apparent in her voice. "It's Nicolette Ryan."

"Oh!" For a second Teresa's thoughts froze. She'd known to expect the lifestyle reporter, but in the rush of everything still to do, she'd forgotten today was her arrival date. "Of course. Tell her I'm on my way."

Once Teresa reached the lobby, it was pretty clear where the celebrity stood. The Opulence catered to the sort of people who could afford to charter airplanes and fund lavish weddings, but actors, musicians and other famous people turned into gawking fans just like the rest of the ordinary folks. The beautiful television reporter was signing an autograph for a teenage girl.

Despite the boost from five-inch pumps, Nicolette Ryan was more petite than Teresa expected. She was dressed in a figure-hugging black sheath and stylish cream-colored coat with a shawl collar. Her long black hair framed an oval face with big brown eyes and an engaging smile.

Teresa waited until the beaming girl had raced back to her family before approaching. "Hello, I'm Teresa St. Claire."

"Nicolette Ryan." The two women shook hands. "I'm covering the Richmond fifth anniversary for a lifestyle piece."

"We've been expecting you. Are you checked in?"

"Yes, but I wanted to touch base with you before I headed up to the room."

"What can I help you with?"

"I wanted to make sure everything was ready for us. I was promised a small breakout room we could use to store our camera equipment and conduct interviews."

"Absolutely. It's all set up." Teresa relaxed. She'd double-checked the space that morning. "Do you want to see it now?"

"Sure…" Her phone started ringing. "I have to take this. Can you give me ten minutes?"

When Nicolette walked off, Teresa turned her attention back to Isabel. The day before she'd laid into the younger woman about Shane. It hadn't been any of her business and she needed to apologize.

"Listen," Teresa began, "what I said yesterday about you and Shane was unfair."

Isabel grimaced. "No, you were right."

"Oh dear," Teresa said, tilting her head in sympathy. "I've seen that look before."

Every day in the mirror since she'd spent the night on Liam's yacht. It was the face of a woman dealing with disappointment. One whose romantic dreams had been slapped down. And heart trampled on.

"I think this is the part where you say, 'I told you so,'" Isabel responded, her customary high spirits dampened.

"I don't want to say, 'I told you so.'" Over a glass of wine in her room last night, Teresa had decided to be happy that Isabel had such faith in what was going on between her and Shane. Being jealous of the other woman's happiness was no excuse for raining on her parade. "I was rude and wrong and I should never have interfered." Although the busy lobby was neither the time nor the place for a heart-to-heart, she liked Isabel and wanted her to know if she needed a shoulder to cry on, Teresa would be there. "Do you want to talk about it? I know I was bitchy and unsympathetic before, but I was wrong."

Isabel's lips tightened as she shook her head. "You weren't wrong. You had Shane figured out. I just didn't want to listen. I wish I had."

"No. I was wrong." The last thing Teresa wanted was for her bad attitude to shadow Isabel's optimism. "I saw you two together. He is completely infatuated with you."

"I don't know about infatuated," Isabel said. "Definitely attracted, but you were right that sex isn't enough and that he's always going to put his career over everything else. Especially a woman he'd only just started getting to know." She looked positively grim as she finished, "And as usual, I moved too fast."

"Don't lose hope," Teresa insisted, wondering at the wisdom of offering romantic advice. "I can't tell you that it will work out between you, but he deserves another shot. It's a lot to expect that Shane would just wake up one morning and be ready for an intense relationship that turns everything he ever thought he wanted and needed on its head."

Yet isn't that what had happened to her? All it had taken was one incredible kiss from Liam to detour her from her carefully mapped-out life.

"Maybe," Isabel said. "But I'm not sure I'll have the chance to find out. I think I'm going to end up leaving the hotel."

That was good news in Teresa's mind. Isabel Withers had a knack for dealing with difficult people and challenging situations, rivaling Teresa in her ability to find solutions to problems.

Teresa smiled and her expression caught Isabel off guard. "I'm not sorry to hear that."

"I don't understand," Isabel said.

"I've been watching you these last few weeks, and you are one of the most organized and creative people I've ever met. Everything I've needed you've anticipated. In my opinion, your talents are wasted here."

Teresa wondered what it would take to hire the concierge away from the hotel.

"That's really nice of you to say." Isabel looked hopeful. "I don't suppose you'd be a reference for me when I go apply for my next position."

"I'll do better than that. I'll hire you."

"Really?"

"You're the exact sort of person I need. Once we're done with the Richmond retreat, let's grab a drink and talk about it."

"I'd like that." Isabel smiled, her relief showing. "But I can't make any promises. I've been so focused on my romantic destination project for The Opulence, I haven't thought what my next career move will be."

"I get that. And I understand if you change your mind about leaving. Especially if things work out between you and Shane."

"They won't."

Teresa saw the pain that flashed across Isabel's face. "They might."

"I'm not leaving because it didn't work out between us. At least not in the way you think." And then Isabel went into a brief explanation about what transpired with the romance concierge idea. "He knew how important the romance concierge idea was to me, and I just don't know if I can stay while someone else does the job that I created."

"That's crappy," Teresa said, genuinely surprised that Shane had handled things so poorly, especially after the way she'd seen him look at Isabel. "We definitely need to get together and talk next week."

"I'd like that."

Nicolette Ryan approached, a warm smile on her face. "I'm ready if you are."

Teresa led the way toward the breakout room she'd assigned to the news crew. "I've seen you interviewing celebrities on the red carpet," she told the reporter. "You have a knack for asking the right questions and putting them at ease."

"I hope I don't disappoint in person."

"Actually, now that I've met you, I think you're even more remarkable."

The woman's smile became a little self-conscious as if she wasn't used to being flattered. If Teresa had been impressed before, this surprising glimpse of the reporter's true nature turned Teresa into a superfan. No wonder that teenage girl had been beaming.

"You're quite beautiful yourself," Nicolette said. "I hope you'll let me get you on camera. I'd love to get a little behind-the-scenes insight on what goes into putting on an event like this."

"I'd be happy to be interviewed." Wasn't that the truth. Exposure like this could only be good for Limitless Events. Too late she remembered Joshua and the troubles he'd gotten himself into. She couldn't afford to have a reporter finding out what she'd done to help out her brother. Or getting wind of the favor she still owed the Fixer. Something like that could ruin her.

"Wonderful," Nicolette said. "I'll set something up with you in the next few days."

"Great." Teresa smiled, but her heart wasn't in it.

As Teresa and Nicolette parted ways, Teresa tabled the potential threat of a curious reporter asking questions she didn't want to answer.

* * *

Although the king-sized bed in Liam's suite was comfortable enough, he had trouble sleeping. Too many thoughts rattled around in his head. Not the least of which was the constant reminder that he'd been planning to share the space with Teresa.

Not long after dawn he was up, showered and heading to the restaurant. He wasn't surprised to spy Teresa seated in the lobby, sipping from a cup and typing on her phone. In the final days before the retreat she'd seemed to be all over the hotel, taking care of the last minute details. Although early on he'd been skeptical of her abilities and had tried to convince Matt to fire her from the event, Liam had to admit he'd been wrong. No matter what had gone on between them, Teresa was a consummate professional and damn good at what she did.

Pushing aside the discomforting flash of admiration, Liam recalled the mission he'd given himself in the days since learning the content of his father's will. At their last encounter, he hadn't made his position known. This time he had no intention of letting her get away until he'd laid out his objectives.

When he drew within ten feet of her, Teresa's attention snapped to him as if aware he was bearing down on her like a tidal wave. Her eyes went wide and her mouth tightened into a flat line as she got to her feet.

"We need to talk about the shares my father left you," he stated, jumping in without polite preliminaries.

Teresa sighed. "What about them?"

"It's important that the shares stay in the family, so I'm having my lawyer draft a contract for you to sign."

"What sort of contract?" Although nothing obvious changed in her body language, her manner became as distant and as cool as a mountain lake.

"A sales contract."

Her eyebrows rose, acknowledging that she had some power in this negotiation. "What if I'm not interested in selling?"

"I will make you a fair offer," he retorted, an edge to his voice. Her willfulness was something he should've prepared for, but hadn't. "As far as I'm concerned, you don't deserve anything from my family."

Now he'd well and truly gotten her back up. "Your father seemed to think otherwise."

Liam ground his teeth in frustration at the position he found himself in. He wasn't accustomed to negotiating with his hands tied. Usually he was operating from a position of strength. Having to come to Teresa when she was obviously up to no good and persuade her to sell to him her shares of stock pained him.

"Look, I don't know what was going on between you and my father—"

"For the last time, nothing was going on—"

"—but for the good of Christopher Corporation, I need control of those shares."

He'd just intimated she wasn't good for Christopher Corporation, and that might not be completely accurate. His father wasn't a fool. He never would've risked the company he'd built by putting it in the hands of someone undeserving.

Unfortunately, Liam wasn't in a place where he could trust anyone. Even the man he'd looked up to every day of his life.

Teresa looked like a thundercloud as she absorbed Liam's censure. "And you thought by coming here and bullying me that I'd happily turn them over?"

"You'll be compensated." This conversation wasn't getting him any closer to his objective, but he couldn't seem to calm the emotions roiling in him.

He didn't want to doubt Teresa. He wanted to sweep her into his arms and find a quiet corner where he could reacquaint himself with all the delightful, impassioned sounds she made when aroused.

"Your father wanted me to have the shares. Aren't you curious why?" She crossed her arms over her chest and looked down her nose at him. "I know I am."

No. Yes.

The question tormented him. He knew his father well. Teresa was a mystery. Yet his father's decision to gift her shares of Christopher Corporation and make her a mandatory board member for a year was beyond Liam's understanding.

"I've been able to think of little else." He made no attempt to hide his suspicion. "I'd very much like to know how you schemed your way into his life. Was it blackmail?"

Far from seeming shocked or angry at his accusation, she shook her head, her entire manner radiating disappointment.

"You can't see the good in anyone, can you?"

Her words acted like a slap, waking him to just how

badly he'd overplayed his hand. Any notion of finess-
ing the truth out of her vanished.

"I see the good in lots of people," he countered, all
too aware how long it took before he fully trusted those
in his orbit.

"Name one," she challenged him.

It wasn't like he thought everyone was out to cheat
him, but he tended to expect everyone was working an
angle. If they were nice to him he wondered what they
wanted. And wasn't it the case that most people were
only looking out for number one? He paid his employees well, knowing that money could buy loyalty. When
it came to business, he made sure all his contracts were
free of loopholes, and he never assumed someone would
help them out just to be nice. If he wanted something
done, he paid for it. An even, clear-cut exchange, spelled
out in black and white, allowed him to sleep nights.

"I'm not playing this game with you." He ignored
her I-told-you-so expression.

Her phone rang before she could respond and she
glanced at the screen, where Matt Richmond's face was
displayed. Worry flickered over her features a second
before she answered.

"Hi, Matt," she said in a breezy, competent tone at
complete odds with the tension she'd displayed with
Liam seconds earlier. "How are you doing?"

She listened and nodded for a few seconds, a genuine
smile kicking up one corner of her mouth at whatever
news the CEO was relaying. Liam didn't realize he had
leaned closer, angling to listen in on Matt's side of the
conversation, until Teresa shot him a peevish glance.

The pallor of her skin and the dark circles beneath her eyes spoke to her exhaustion. She wasn't as invincible as she wanted everyone to think. For some reason this stirred his sympathy. With her defenses fraying, he should be going in for the kill. Instead he found himself wanting to pitch in and help.

"Everything is going smoothly here. In fact, we are ahead of schedule."

This lie, told with absolute conviction, rocked Liam back on his heels and reminded him that what came out of her mouth wasn't always the truth.

"You and Nadia have fun," Teresa said, seeing Liam's expression and making a face at him. "Don't worry about anything. I have everything under control." She was smiling at Matt's final words as she ended the call. Without a beat she pointed her finger at Liam. "I know what you're thinking, but don't say it. Matt is on his honeymoon. You don't seriously expect me to burden him with things he can't control, do you?"

"And when he shows up and finds Jessie won't be singing for his guests?"

Teresa tossed her head. "Jessie will come through. She signed a very lucrative contract."

"Yes," he mused. "Money talks."

Teresa shook her head. "You know, before you showed up here with your sales contracts and insults, I was debating whether to accept or refuse what your father left me."

Liam's skepticism must've shown because she sighed heavily and seemed to deflate. Where only a moment ago outrage had enhanced her energy, making her seem invincible, now she looked vulnerable and lost as she scanned his features.

"And now?"

"I only want to make things better for you." She took a half step forward until he could feel the heat of her skin so close, so fragrant, so damned soft. "It's too bad you haven't figured that out yet."

She lifted her hand, the movement slow and dreamy, but before her fingertips could touch his cheek, he caught her wrist. Touching her stirred his blood and roused his emotions. Anger. Lust. Longing. Even as he rejected her sympathy, he wanted to pull her soft curves against his rigid muscles. To kiss her senseless and feel her melt into him. To hear her moan and beg for more.

Somber eyes searched his expression. Did she hope to find pity or mercy? The conflicting emotions in her eyes reflected his pain and confusion. For an instant he was transported back in time. To when their hearts had beat as one. She'd seen through his defenses. Glimpsed the hunger for more than just sex. For connection. For love.

Their gazes locked. Held. Broke away. Each retreating as self-preservation took over.

"I have work to do," she declared breathlessly, turning and rushing off without another word, leaving Liam staring after her, regret dominating his emotions.

Idiot.

He pivoted in the opposite direction, refusing to watch her go, biting down hard on the words that would stop her retreat, bring her back to him.

Nine

Shane prowled through The Opulence's lobby, his attention only partially focused on the phone in his hand. It had been several days since the night he and Isabel had spent together and they'd exchanged only one abbreviated personal text and several professional conversations about the looming Richmond retreat.

Usually few women lingered in his thoughts after a sexual interlude. Mostly he enjoyed their company in the moment and went back to thinking about work. That should've been the case even more so right now with the enormous spotlight being focused on The Opulence thanks to the important event they were hosting for his division's parent company.

Instead, he'd found his thoughts drifting back to the night he'd spent with Isabel at the most inopportune time. This development left him feeling raw and out of sorts, yet dwelling on her made him so damned happy. His seesawing emotions filled him with indecision about how to proceed.

He hadn't intended to complicate his life by sleeping with one of his employees. The fact that he was irresistibly drawn to Isabel wasn't an excuse for such a breach in professionalism. Now that he'd crossed that line, he should man up and tell her that it couldn't happen again.

If only he could trust himself to keep that promise.

"Shane." A male voice broke into his thoughts, turning him in the direction of the hail.

Spying Liam Christopher, Shane extended his hand to his boss's best friend. "How is it going?"

"I'll be doing better once the Richmond party gets going," Liam said. "I imagine you feel the same way."

Shane nodded. "So much is riding on everything going smoothly."

"Do you have time to grab a drink with me?" Liam nodded toward the bar.

"Sure." Out of the corner of his eye, Shane spotted Isabel emerging from the offices behind the front desk. Shane noticed that Isabel wasn't heading toward the concierge desk. On impulse, he decided to intercept her. "Can you give me a couple minutes? I have some business I need to take care of first."

"I'll see you in there."

Although Isabel was moving with purpose, Shane's long strides let him draw near with very little effort. She looked surprised and not too pleased that he'd slipped through the employee-only exit behind her.

"Are you getting out of here?" he asked, matching her pace, wondering why she didn't stop or even slow.

"Yes," she said. "I'm done for the day."

"I just agreed to have a drink with Liam. Would you have time for dinner later?"

"I'm going out with a friend."

Shane noticed a definite chill in the air and thought he knew the reason. "Look, I'm sorry I haven't been in touch—"

The glance she shot his way was full of reproof. "Do you really think I'm that childish?"

"No." Maybe he was missing something. "Of course not. It's just that I've been busy this week and you probably expected me to call…"

"While it would've been nice to hear from you, I understand that you have a lot going on with the upcoming retreat."

If he took what she said at face value, then why was she so annoyed with him? "What about dinner tomorrow?"

That stopped her. She swung around to face him, her beautiful hazel eyes narrowing as she regarded him. Whatever she saw made her lips tighten.

"I just can't do this with you right now," she said. "I have to go."

Before Shane could sort out what had gone wrong between them since their passionate goodbye kiss a few days earlier, Isabel turned and marched off down the corridor. More puzzled than annoyed, Shane retraced his steps and headed toward the bar.

Liam sat at a table near the window, watching raindrops run like tears down the glass. His drink was nearly empty, and as Shane entered, he signaled to the waitress to bring him a scotch and ordered another round for Liam.

"Everything okay?" Shane asked as he took the seat opposite the head of Christopher Corporation.

"Is this rain ever going to stop?"

"The forecast isn't looking good." Shane wondered if Liam's melancholy had to do with the persistent storm or the recent loss of his father.

"Matt's going to be pissed if this affects turnout for the retreat. He wanted to go big for the fifth anniversary."

Shane had been thinking the same thing. "Have you heard from him?"

Liam finished his drink before answering. "He and Nadia got married on a beach somewhere in the Caribbean. He sent me this." Liam showed Shane a picture of Matt sweeping his lovely bride into a romantic kiss.

All Shane could think as he stared at the photo was that Isabel would've loved how that unexpected romance had turned out. "She was his assistant."

"Yep." Liam turned the phone around and stared morosely at the picture.

"Seems like he crossed a line professionally."

"I guess."

The waitress set drinks down in front of the two men and scooped up Liam's empty glass. The interruption gave Shane several seconds to ponder this development.

"He must've figured she was the one for him," Shane

continued, unable to stop himself from musing out loud. "But how did he know?"

Liam was contemplating the ice in his drink, his frown making it appear as if he was only listening with half his attention. "I've been wondering the same thing myself since I got the news. I never imagined Matt was looking to settle down. And now that he has…"

"What about you?" Shane asked, remembering Isabel mentioning that a certain event planner had caught Liam's eye. "It seems like you and Teresa St. Claire were hitting it off."

"That's over." Liam spun his glass on the table. "She wasn't the person I thought she was."

"Sorry to hear that." And to Shane's surprise, he did feel bad for Liam.

It occurred to Shane that ten days ago he never would've given any relationship a second thought, failed or successful. He'd been one hundred percent focused on the portfolio of hotels managed by his division. Now, he caught himself daydreaming about an idealistic redhead who'd disrupted his usually organized thoughts with flights of fancy.

"Are you involved with anyone?" Liam asked in turn, but Shane wasn't sure if it was out of politeness or curiosity.

"No time," Shane said, offering his stock answer.

"You should make time." Startling advice coming from a guy as known to be allergic to romantic entanglements as Liam Christopher.

"You can say that after your thing with Teresa didn't work out?"

Liam shrugged. "It was great while it lasted."

"So you're thinking you'll be more open to a relationship next time around?"

"I wouldn't go that far." Liam smirked, but the smile never touched his eyes. "Right now all I'm thinking about is the Richmond event and the announcement I'm set to make Saturday morning."

"Sure." With a nod, Shane let the thread drop.

In fact, he had no idea why he'd pursued the topic for as long as he had. It's not like he was thinking about getting married and looking for reasons why he should keep seeing Isabel. A wife and kids were a distraction his career couldn't afford. Maybe he'd be open if she was the sort of woman who would be satisfied with financial security and the perks of being an executive's wife. Someone who'd accept his ridiculous hours and not make undue demands on his time.

That was not Isabel Withers. From the beginning, she'd been bossy, cajoling, impossible to ignore. She'd keep on influencing every aspect of his life, from what he ate to how he exercised. She'd encourage him to take up hobbies. Suggest activities they could do together. She enjoyed hiking. No doubt they'd hit the trails on the weekends. To take in the scenery. To relax. He could see them getting a dog. Yet another thing to make demands on his attention.

Shane didn't have time for any of that. He was on a mission to make his father eat his words. And Isabel was in the way. Getting involved with her had already put his career in jeopardy. The smart move would be to end things before any permanent damage was done.

Seeing that Liam's attention had drifted to the rain-filled evening outside, Shane picked up his phone and sent a text.

We need to talk.

Jacked up on caffeine and frustration, Teresa tapped her foot as she waited for her coffee order to be filled. Her phone buzzed as texts poured in. With two days until the retreat began, she should've been completely focused on the event, but found herself in a state of near constant distraction because of Liam's presence at the hotel.

It seemed as if fate conspired to put him in her path at every turn. She recognized that made sense since he was acting as Matt's right hand while the Richmond Enterprises CEO was enjoying his honeymoon, but every time she ran into him, she recalled her behavior during their last encounter.

Had she really been so naive as to think that letting him glimpse how much she cared about him might make all his animosity and mistrust go away? Worse, she'd been surprised when he'd rejected her olive branch. Then there was the impending contract he'd insisted she sign, promising to sell him her shares in the company at the end of a year. She continued to vacillate over what to do about that.

With Liam at the helm and thanks to the deal he'd recently made with Richmond Enterprises with the joint venture, the Sasha project, it sounded as if Christopher Corporation was going to become even more success-ful than it already was. Part of her wanted to keep the shares and grow wealthy beyond what she'd ever imagined possible.

On the other hand, her financial problems clamored for her to sell the shares to Liam. The money could then be used to help her brother, who seemed to be constantly in debt. Then too, a single signature could vanquish those nagging fears that she was one calamity away from bankrupting her company.

She took her coffee and thanked the barista. Her knotted shoulder muscles loosened somewhat as she pondered having a financial cushion. How wonderful it would be to have the flexibility to take only those clients who appreciated her talent and expertise and the benefit to her business if she could focus on what she did best.

With a sigh, Teresa brought her attention back to the text one of her staff had sent. The florist ordered the wrong shade of lilies. They're pink not yellow. This was a fall event. She'd wanted the guest room bouquets to reflect the glorious autumn tones of the maples, oaks and aspens. Why couldn't anything in her life go smoothly? Her phone picked that moment to ring. Glancing at the familiar number, she braced herself before answering.

"Tell me it's good news for a change," she said to Isabel Withers.

"Jessie Humphrey just arrived!" The concierge's wild exuberance came through loud and clear. Isabel had proclaimed herself a huge fan when Teresa asked her to be on the lookout for the singer.

"I'm on my way."

With the steady sheets of rain falling outside, the activity at the front desk had ground to a halt, allow-ing all three staff members to cluster before a lean, sexy woman wearing jeans and a gray sweater beneath an oversized black trench coat. Although Jessie was known for her impeccable taste in heels, today she wore sensible black boots, perfect for traveling in that day's drenching downpour.

Teresa approached the new arrival, admiring the woman's perfect caramel-colored skin and lustrous dark brown curls piled atop her head before introducing herself.

"I'm so glad you made it," Teresa added, wondering what miracle had changed Jessie's mind about traveling in the terrible weather. "Did you have any trouble getting here?"

"I was a little worried about traveling by helicopter," Jessie said, sliding off her dark glasses, her white smile flashing. "But then I realized that the coast guard uses them all the time to rescue people during storms. And the pilot was so confident that I relaxed."

"That was so smart of you to hire a helicopter," Teresa said, wondering how many other guests would arrive that way. After all, the hotel was an hour's car ride from Seattle, but the roads would be challenging to navigate during the storms.

"It wasn't me. The arrangements were made by Christopher Corporation. I understand they have something to do with the event this weekend."

Teresa's brain felt sluggish as she absorbed this information. "Liam Christopher?"

"I believe that's right." Jessie gave a little shrug. "Do you know him?"

Did she? Obviously not as well as she thought.

"Yes." Her throat seized up. Liam had arranged for Jessie to arrive on time and safely. Had he done it for her or to keep Matt from being disappointed? More likely the latter since he hadn't said anything to her about it. Should she be annoyed with him or grateful? "I'll let him know you've arrived. After you settle into your suite, I'll show you where you will be performing. Meanwhile, if there's anything you need, Isabel is our concierge." Teresa cracked a smile. "And a huge fan."

Teresa was feeling far more hopeful by the time she'd returned to the concierge desk. Maybe things were starting to take a turn for the better. "Well, that's certainly a relief."

Isabel smiled at her. "You know, I think there's a spa appointment with your name on it tonight at six."

"Oh, I couldn't." But the thought of taking a couple hours off to be pampered was almost more than she could resist.

"If you don't slow down you'll burn out before the retreat even starts."

"I couldn't possibly..." But Teresa could feel herself weakening. She gripped her smartphone until her fingers cramped. So many details awaited her attention. "I really shouldn't..."

Before she could offer another weak protest, Isabel pushed an appointment card across the desk in her direction.

"Six o'clock," the concierge repeated. "You'll be getting an oxygenating facial followed by our famous Desert Sage Massage. Don't be late."

* * *

Fresh off the spa's Turkish Hammam ritual, Liam stepped into a room with the dual massage tables and shut the door behind him. He hadn't known what to expect from the rub and scrub experience, but found the Turkish water treatment unusual but enjoyable. He'd lain face down on a hot marble bed while water had been poured over his legs and back. A couple of rounds of soapy scrub had followed, and then a shower of water waved back and forth had rinsed him clean. After drying off and donning his robe, he'd been escorted to this room.

Soothing music filled the candlelit space. Staged beside the wall to his left sat two comfortable chairs with a round table between. A champagne bottle chilled in a bucket with two flutes beside it. One empty. One filled. Lifting the full glass to his lips, he tossed back half the liquid, feeling the prickle of bubbles exploding against the back of his throat.

He stripped off his robe and let it fall across the arm of one of the chairs. Naked, he approached the nearest massage table, noting the tightness in his shoulders put there since reading his father's will. Caught up in his thoughts, Liam didn't realize the second bed was occupied until he neared the sheet-shrouded tables.

Two massage beds.

Champagne with two flutes.

What the hell? Had he been directed to the wrong room?

In his confusion he must've made a sound because the mound beneath the linens shifted. A woman's bare arm appeared, hand clutching the linen covering to her chest. She awkwardly shifted onto her elbow to prop up her upper body. Familiar features shifted from shock to dismay as Teresa spied him.

She squeaked and recoiled, but trapped by the sheets and her unwillingness to risk exposure, she had nowhere to go. "What the hell are you doing here?"

The full impact that they were both naked and very much alone landed a direct punch. He swallowed hard. "I'm here for a massage." His voice came out more husky than he liked.

His explanation sent her gaze roaming over his bare torso. His lower half was mostly hidden by the massage table, but part of him was slowly rising into view as his lust awoke with a gleeful howl.

Teresa stared at him, her mouth working but no sound coming out. Her fixation on his body only increased the rush of blood to his groin. The impulse to leap across the table and haul her into his arms grew stronger with each thunderous beat of his heart. What kept him in place wasn't his suspicions about her relationship with his father or her earlier refusal to sell him the Christopher Corporation shares, but the knowledge that they could be interrupted at any moment.

"You can't be," she said in a breathless rush. "I'm here for a massage. You must be in the wrong room."

"No," he countered, sensing mischief at work. The hotel functioned too efficiently for this to have been a mistake. "This is where I was directed. Obviously someone thought we might enjoy a couple's massage."

"Don't be ridiculous. We're the farthest thing from a couple."

And then he recalled that he'd intended to romance her during the Richmond retreat before finding out about his father's will and had never ordered his assistant to cancel the arrangements.

Annoyed at the absurd situation, he lifted the top sheet. "You've got that right."

Still…now that he was here…

Sliding between the sheets, he settled onto the table, biting back a groan as the warmth from the heated bed enveloped him in a comfortable embrace. Despite the hotel's air being a perfect balance of temperature and humidity, the rainy November weather seemed to have worked its chill into his bones and muscles.

"What do you think you're doing?" Teresa demanded. "You can't stay here."

"I told you. I'm here for a massage." He turned his head and regarded her with a half smile. "If that makes you uncomfortable, feel free to leave."

Of course, she'd have to parade her naked body past him to reach her robe, which he'd belatedly realized was hanging from a hook on the back of the door, and he'd definitely lift his head to watch the show.

"Look," he said, "It's just a massage."

"A couple's massage," she fumed.

He ignored the interruption. "I think both of us could use a little relaxation right about now." With a muted huff, she settled back down, and over the tinkling chimes and water sounds coming from the stereo speakers, he heard the shuffling sounds of her straightening the linens.

Seconds later a soft knock sounded on the door and a pair of women entered. They introduced themselves as Diane and April. Soon, the scent of lavender and bergamot filled the air as the massage therapists began working essential oils into their skin.

To Liam's relief, the pair worked in silence, offering him a chance to fully immerse himself in the pleasure of strong fingers digging deep into his tight muscles. As he lost himself to Diane's competent hands it became possible to put Teresa out of his mind and let himself float, but when the time came to turn onto his stomach, he couldn't help but glance her way to see how she was enjoying the experience.

Was it a coincidence that she'd brought her attention to bear on him at the exact same moment? Their gazes collided and sparks raced along his nerve endings. He spied the turmoil in her eyes, noted a similar uproar pushing aside his earlier tranquility.

Craving her. Distrusting her. Fighting emotions that should've died when she inherited the Christopher Corporation shares. His body and mind were at complete odds. But it was his heart—unreliable, traitorous organ—that he couldn't control.

Ten

Teresa tore her gaze away from the questions roiling in Liam's eyes, unable to believe she was lying naked on a massage table a mere three feet away from him. For the last half an hour she'd been kicking herself for staying. Why hadn't she gotten up and left the room? She couldn't blame modesty. The man had seen her naked before. Plus, she could have wrapped herself in the sheet and avoided flashing him.

She'd stayed out of sheer stubbornness. Unwilling to give him the satisfaction of having driven her away. Refusing to let him know how strongly he affected her.

It wasn't fair that he stirred her body and made her heart seize with longing. Her whole body ached that she'd chosen a man whose distrust flared at the slightest provocation. And yet, had she chosen him?

Did her yearning for Liam Christopher make any sense?

Sure, she admired his business acumen and appreciated his incredible body. His charisma had bowled her over, but she was sensible enough to resist any of those things. What had gotten to her was the way he'd jumped in and helped her brother without being asked. He hadn't needed to get involved. He wasn't trying to win her over or seduce her. Unlike the Fixer, there'd been no demand of a future payment or expectation that she owed him a favor in return. Nor did she doubt that he'd taken on just such a thing on her behalf.

The massage therapist dug strong fingers into Teresa's tight shoulders and the delicious pain made her bite back a moan. Until April started working on her back, Teresa hadn't realized just how knotted up she'd become. When was the last time she'd treated herself to a massage? A year? Why couldn't she bring herself to take time to relax? Because she was always chasing the win, never quite believing that her work would be good enough.

Teresa forced away thoughts of Liam and work and concentrated on letting her muscles unwind. She was almost asleep by the time the hour was up and the two women slipped from the room. Loathing the return to reality, but recognizing that the Richmond event wasn't going to organize itself, Teresa sighed. Although the massage therapists said there was no immediate need to evacuate the room, dozens of details still awaited her attention.

The swoosh of the champagne bottle sliding free of

its ice bath disrupted the soothing music that had been playing during the massage. Teresa's eyes flew open. How had she forgotten that she wasn't alone? Clutching the sheet to her bare chest, keenly aware of her nakedness, Teresa levered onto one elbow and watched Liam refill both flutes.

"I'll close my eyes if you want to get up."

Unsure if he was being gallant or sardonic, Teresa glared at him while resentment rumbled. He certainly hadn't been shy about showing off his own body, and she envied his confidence. It would serve him right if she paraded past him in glorious nudity, and before she could question the impulse, she tossed aside the sheet and slid off the massage table.

Head held high, pointedly ignoring him, she ambled over to her robe, lifted it off the hook and slipped into it. Despite the adrenaline hit to her earlier tranquility, her boldness both amazed and pleased her. Buoyed by confidence, she knotted the belt and turned in Liam's direction rather than follow her instincts and bolt out the door.

"Champagne?" he asked smoothly, extending one of the flutes in her direction.

"Thank you." Proud of her unruffled tone, Teresa stepped close enough to take the drink. She lifted it to her lips and took a leisurely sip, debating her next move. "For five minutes, can we pretend that nothing exists outside this room?"

Liam's eyes narrowed and he regarded her with a mixture of wariness and curiosity. "What did you have in mind?"

Something crazy and reckless.

The man's suspicious nature had brought things to an end before she'd been ready to let go. The shock of his rejection had left her floundering with a dozen declarations unsaid. Their last night together had been ripe with promise and she'd been eager to take their relationship in the direction of deeper intimacy. In the aftermath of that fateful evening, she'd been angry and confused, but mostly she'd been frustrated because while he might have received closure that night, she'd been too busy defending herself to have the same.

Teresa set her glass on the table, hoping she hadn't misread his signals. "What I had in mind…" she said, avoiding his gaze lest she see something reflected in his eyes that stopped her cold. Heart thumping vigorously against her ribs, she narrowed the distance between them. With fingers that shook, she raked her nails into his hair in the way she knew he liked. "…is this."

The tension knotted in her stomach as he set aside his glass and wrapped his arms around her, stopping her breath. Tears burned her eyes that he hadn't rejected her advance. The hard embrace gave her no space and no chance to reinflate her lungs before his lips crashed down on hers.

Moaning beneath the delicious hunger of his kiss, she opened to his questing tongue and met his passion with fierce joy. No matter what else was wrong between them, this all-consuming desire would always burn white-hot and pure.

When his hand slipped between them and tugged open her robe, she didn't protest. His palm skimmed over her hip and rode the indention of her waist to her breast. Lowering his head, he took one nipple into his mouth and sucked. She gasped as the sexy tug sent a bolt of electricity straight through her. Her world shimmered with pleasure from that alone, but then his hand was sliding between her thighs and he was dropping to his knees before her.

His lips skimmed over the twitching muscles of her abdomen and moved lower. "You are so beautiful," he muttered, his tone reverent, as he ran his palms along the backs of her thighs.

He kissed her legs with such adoration that Teresa wanted to cry out from that alone. All of the arguments and anger melted away as she plummeted into a world of white-hot desire.

"I have to taste you," he murmured against her skin. "I haven't been able to stop thinking about you. Let me. Just let me do this for you."

Teresa couldn't say no to that request. Especially not after the way he asked. The husky, aching throb in his voice left her wet and achy and hot. Earlier, while the massage therapist had worked lotion over her skin, she'd imagined it was Liam's hands stroking her shoulders and sliding along her legs. Nearly purring with pleasure, she'd taken the fantasy one step further and pictured his fingers easing into the dampness between her thighs, stroking her the way she loved.

The hunger aroused by the vision had been almost too much to bear. She'd never imagined he'd ever want to touch her like that again. Yet here he was, tending to her needs as if he'd read her mind and teased forth all her imaginings.

Her knees buckled as his tongue slid across where she wanted him most. He gripped her hips, anchoring her while she threaded her fingers through his hair. She gasped his name as he deepened the masterful stroke of his tongue. Shaking, lit up like a Fourth of July celebration from the pleasure of his deft touch, she moaned and murmured, encouraging him while waves of pleasure pummeled her.

"You taste so good," he whispered before returning to her slick heat, lapping at her clit, turning her world upside down with jolt after jolt of sharp, blissful sensation.

Shamelessly, she grabbed his head, pulling him closer. Her pleasure tightened and escalated, intensifying to such an extent that she rocked her hips into his face, pressing herself against his mouth, while a soft frantic keening escaped her parted lips. He seemed to understand that she was close because he pulled her even tighter against him, fingers digging into her soft bottom, touching off the electric spark that started the chain reaction of her climax. Oblivious that the massage room was neither isolated nor soundproof, she held nothing back. Her wild cries sounded frantic and desperate as shockwaves rolled over her.

Gasping for air, her legs trembling so badly she could scarcely stand, she relaxed her fingers and stroked Liam's dark head in appreciation. He set his forehead against her abdomen, hands continuing to coast from the back of her knees to the small of her back, tender caresses so unlike the heated tight grip on her moments earlier.

"That was amazing," she rasped, making no attempt to hide her admiration. Wanting to return the pleasure, she began to sink down. "Let me do that for you."

"No." He lunged to his feet and grabbed her arms beneath the elbows, keeping her upright. He wouldn't meet her eyes as he growled, "This was a mistake."

She wanted to scream denials at him. To insist that the only mistake was that he doubted her. But humiliation pressed on her vocal chords, muting her. She could only shake her head, denying his claim.

"Liam…"

"I can't keep doing this," he said, cutting her off.

"Keep doing what?" His declaration left her reeling. How could he be like this after what had just happened between them? After the care he'd taken with her pleasure?

"Encounters like this aren't good for either of us. We have to move on."

As if she'd been pushed into icy water, she began to shake. After tearing her arms from his grasp, Teresa snatched her robe together and fumbled with the belt.

That's what she'd been trying to do. To close a door. One last kiss goodbye.

"Don't you think I want to?" she countered, knowing how ridiculous she sounded. She'd made the move on him, practically begged him for a kiss. No wonder he was confused.

"I don't know what you want."

I want you.

But she recognized that even if she spoke the words out loud he wouldn't care. He'd made up his mind about her and no amount of arguing would change his opinion. Instead of making an even bigger fool of herself, she slumped into the nearby chair in miserable silence while Liam headed for the door. The idealistic part of her that couldn't stop believing they were meant to be together wanted to call out, to ask him not to go, but she bit her lip and stubbornly held her tongue. As much as she longed to recapture the connection that had been growing between them before they'd discovered the terms of his father's will, Teresa wasn't sure that was possible.

Isabel stood at the bathroom sink of her tiny cabin and stared at the text Shane had sent her the previous night. She could guess what was on his mind. This has been fun, baby, but I don't have time for you. Although it wasn't in her nature to play games, the brusque message had vexed her and so she was taking her time responding. The delay hadn't enabled her to calm down and think rationally, but no matter how angry, it went against her nature to be bitchy and rude.

I'm off at four.

She'd debated beating him to the punch and ending things via text, but wanted to see his face as he dropped his bomb on her. On the heels of her reply came another message.

Are you available for dinner tonight?

Outrageous. How could he act as if the whole Camilla Maxwell situation wasn't eating her alive? After the lengths she'd gone to, showing him the candlelit proposal on the bridge and the romantic photo shoot in front of the falls, he should've known she'd be devastated to be passed over. He deserved to get a lengthy lecture on how people deserved to be treated, and that required time and privacy.

Sure. I'll cook.

She followed up with her address and brief directions. Hosting him at the cabin she rented was strategic. She wanted privacy to speak her mind, and if he needed to escape, it would be less awkward if he didn't have to stick around to settle the bill.

In the hours that followed, Isabel had waffled between anxiety and righteous frustration. After work she'd shopped for groceries and did some last-minute tidying up while practicing her impassioned lecture. As the clock ticked past seven and the rain continued to drench the area, Isabel wondered if Shane had sensed the hell storm he was about to walk into and changed his mind about coming, or if he was merely having trouble finding the place. A mixed bag of relief and annoyance rushed through her as she spied headlights winding up her driveway.

Heart drumming in time with the downpour, she went to the door and flung it open to watch him approach. Raindrops sparkled on his dark hair and the shoulders of his trench coat as he took her porch steps in two easy bounds and came to stand before her. His enticing lips bore no sign of a smile. Despite the bottle of wine he extended toward her, he looked as if he was approaching tonight's dinner as a business meeting.

"Did you have trouble finding the place?" she asked, her dread twisting in her stomach as she fell back and motioned him inside.

"I missed the turn the first time," he said. "You're pretty isolated here."

"I love being surrounded by all the trees." She forced a smile. "It means I don't have a view, but I really enjoy the solitude."

"You strike me as the sort who would rather be in the thick of things in the middle of town."

Against her better judgment, his remark warmed her. He'd been thinking about her. She liked that far too much.

"Let me take your coat."

While she hung the trench coat on a hook near her door, he surveyed the pine-covered walls, tiny living room and ancient but clean kitchen. His expression gave no clue what he thought of the deer antler side tables, the worn couch covered by one of her mother's quilting projects or the cheery fire crackling in the stone fireplace. While the ambiance might not be up to his standards, the meal she'd prepared was one from her favorite food blogger and destined to impress.

"Something smells really good," he remarked, his keen gaze on her as she moved into the kitchen.

Satisfaction bloomed. She was eager to demonstrate her skills to him once again. In the wake of her meeting with Tom, Isabel wanted Shane to realize he'd made a mistake in choosing Camilla Maxwell over her as romance concierge.

"It's a standing rib roast," she told him.

"Can I help you with anything?"

He dominated her small space with his tall, muscular form and powerful personality. Tonight he'd exchanged his expensive business suit for worn jeans and a navy sweater.

In the grip of an awkward bout of nerves, she gestured to the bottle. "You can open the wine."

She pulled out a corkscrew and handed it over. She watched him work while Jessie Humphrey's voice flowed from a Bluetooth speaker in the living room. The romantic music was a mistake. Her phone was on the counter and she tapped to skip the song.

As many times as she'd seen the star performing on TV, for some reason now that she'd met Jessie, Isabel perceived a whole new level of nuance in Jessie's performance. She sang like her soul had been shredded. Like each word held deep personal meaning. And perhaps they did. For all her fame and fortune, the pain in Jessie Humphrey was real and palpable. Isabel's heart ached in sympathy.

Shane looked up from pouring the wine. "Why'd you change the song?"

Isabel wished she dared tell him the real reason. That she felt betrayed and regretted the feelings she'd developed for him over the last year. "I wasn't in the mood."

One dark eyebrow rose. "It seems like the way she

puts her whole heart in every one of her songs would
be right up your alley."

"Songs with that much emotion are born out of heart-
ache." And too raw for how she was feeling at the moment. "Every time I listen to her I wonder who she's
writing about."

"Hmm," Shane mused. "Another topic you're knowl-
edgeable about. Among your many talents, are you a
songwriter, too?"

"No." Isabel reached for a glass of wine and took a
hearty gulp to dull a sudden flare of pain. "My father
was. He wrote all his own stuff."

"What sort of music?"

"Alternative rock, mostly."

"Would I recognize the group?"

"I doubt it. His band never broke out, but they had a
small but loyal following. Sometimes I think it would've
been better if they'd either hit it big or failed completely."
Isabel wasn't sure why she felt suddenly compelled to
share such a painful part of her life. "My dad was gone
all the time, traveling all over the country, mostly playing smaller venues."

"Why would it have been better if he'd made it big
or failed?"

"If he'd failed, my mother could have convinced
him to give it up. If he'd succeeded he wouldn't have
felt so desperate to keep going. He and his bandmates
were constantly chasing the next big opportunity. It
consumed my father."

She stopped speaking, recalling those complicated

days before her father had stopped coming home to his wife and daughter altogether.

"I know what it's like to work too hard, chasing something that doesn't exist," Shane said, his eyes on a distant place, a muscle jumping in his jaw. "Ever since I graduated from college and my dad told me I wasn't good enough to join the family business, I've sacrificed everything to prove him wrong."

"Seems to me that you accomplished what you set out to do. No one looking at you and seeing all you've done would be anything but proud of you."

"Yet that's not the case. My dad will never see me as anything but the screwup I was all through high school and into college."

"I can't imagine that's true. The *Seattle Business Journal* named you one of the city's rising stars. Surely he saw the article."

"Oh, he saw it. My uncle made certain of that. But he never said a word to me."

Despite his stoic expression, Shane's pain came through loud and clear. Impulsively, Isabel reached for his hand. When Shane squeezed her fingers in return, Isabel found in him a sympathetic soul.

"The night my dad left for good, I heard him tell my mother how he wished I'd never been born." The confession surprised Isabel. It was something she'd only ever shared with her closest friends.

"Come here." Shane pulled her into his arms and dropped his cheek against the top of her head.

When she'd pictured how the night would go, she'd never expected that sharing her story with Shane and

hearing his in return would take some of the sting out
of her father's leaving. Nor had she intended to end up
in his arms. The ache in her throat impressed on Isabel how complicated their situation was. Shane had the
power to ruin her career and damage her heart.

"I guess we should both give up on our fathers ever
loving us the way we want," she murmured against his
chest, telling herself to stop being a fool. She shouldn't
be taking solace from past hurts in Shane's arms after
the way he'd let her down about the romance concierge
position. At last she rallied her willpower and pushed
away. "I can't do this."

"Do what?" When she didn't immediately answer,
Shane tried again. "Look, if you're upset about what's
been going on, you don't need to be."

How could the man act like replacing her as The Opulence's romance concierge was a nothing event? Did
he seriously think he could encourage her ideas, invite
her to pitch those ideas to corporate marketing, give her
the most amazing night of her life and then act like it
was okay to steal what she'd developed?

"I don't need to be upset?" Isabel couldn't believe
what she was hearing. "You've got to be kidding."

"Okay." Peering at her from beneath his ridiculously
long lashes, he raked his fingers through his hair, disrupting the waves. The dishevelment only increased his
appeal. "I'll admit I'm not good at this."

Was this some sort of master manipulation to make
her look like the crazy, unreasonable one? He couldn't
possibly be as perplexed as he appeared. This sheep-
ish charm had to be a device he used to twist situa-

tions to his advantage, right? Except he hadn't shown himself to be anything less than completely straightforward with her.

"Oh, I think you're plenty good at it," she muttered, refusing to be fooled. "In fact, it seems to me that you've mastered the art of doing exactly this."

"You're wrong." The sound he huffed out sounded like a rusty chuckle. "I've spent my life doing the exact opposite."

Eleven

With tension stretching his nerves to the point of discomfort, Shane watched as Isabel's lush mouth tightened into a grim line. Despite her unhappy expression, she looked so damned adorable in her bare feet, snug jeans and dark green sweater bringing out the forest green in her eyes. He was almost overwhelmed by the impulse to take her to bed and let the dinner burn. But they were in the midst of something that couldn't be solved with hot, sweaty sex.

The problem stemmed from that we-need-to-talk text, signaling that he didn't want to pursue her further. The instant it had left his phone he regretted sending it because as soon as he'd taken steps to shut things down between him and Isabel, Shane recognized that was the last thing he wanted to do. Worse, unaccustomed to owning his emotions, he'd been reluctant to send a follow-up text, explaining his dilemma.

Thus, he'd been overjoyed when she'd agreed to have dinner, hoping maybe she hadn't taken the text the way he'd meant it. But from the way she was reacting right now, his struggle to communicate with Isabel had led to him mucking things up.

"What are you talking about?" she demanded, annoyance bleeding into confusion.

"What am I talking about?" Shane countered, sensing he was walking blindfolded through a minefield. "What are you talking about?"

"Like you don't know." Isabel set her hands on her hips and glared at him.

"I really don't think I do." He leaned back against the kitchen counter and crossed his arms over his chest. "Can you tell me what's going on with you?"

Her scowl grew even more pronounced as she began. "Yesterday, Tom told me that he thinks promoting the hotel as a romance destination has merit and wants to go ahead with it."

"It'll be a huge benefit." Shane nodded, recalling how enthusiastic his marketing department had been. "You were right about that."

"And the romance concierge position?"

"What about it?"

She tossed her head, causing her silky russet locks to drift and resettle. "Are you kidding me?"

A bad feeling grew in his gut. "What's wrong?"

"I'm not going to be The Opulence's romance concierge."

"You're not?" He could see she was unhappy about this. "What's changed?"

"What's changed?" she echoed bitterly. "Like you didn't know that Tom hired Camilla Maxwell to be the face of all things romantic and trendy at the hotel."

This news was a blow Shane didn't see coming. Holy hell. No wonder she was so upset. He lifted his hand, intending to touch her, but she backed out of reach.

"I didn't," he assured her, not convinced she believed him. "And she's a blogger. How would that even work?"

"It'll work because I'm the one who will continue to do the actual work of making the guests' experiences perfect." Isabel's disillusionment ground into Shane like broken glass. "How could you…" she broke off and dashed her knuckles beneath the corners of both eyes.

"How could I what?"

Her breath came and went in huge, unsteady gulps. "Tom said that corporate agreed."

Now he understood why she'd been avoiding him. A string of curses flowed through Shane's thoughts. "I assure you I knew nothing about it."

"You didn't tell him to?" Her misery lost its sharp edges as hope reentered her gaze.

"Of course not." Shane frowned. "And anyway, it doesn't matter."

"And why not?" She shot back. Obviously it mattered to her.

"Because you're not going to be working for The Opulence much longer." Seeing the panic in her hazel eyes, he rushed to explain. "Your talents are wasted on a single hotel. I want to bring you to corporate headquarters. I'd like you to look at every one of the hotels Richmond manages and come up with a romantic plan for each one."

Her eyes opened wide. "That sounds amazing. I never imagined…" She broke off and shifted her gaze away. "This isn't because…"

"Because?"

"We're sleeping together."

"I'd already decided to offer you the position before anything happened between us." That wasn't quite true. When he'd kissed her that first time, he hadn't been thinking of promoting her. He'd just given into the overwhelming urge to taste her. "I'm bringing you to corporate because you sold me on your ideas and the marketing department thought you were brilliant."

She considered this for a long moment before asking, "So, how will this affect things between us?"

Shane didn't have a ready answer. Not only did he recoil from going public about dating one of his employees, but also the way Isabel whipped up his emotions pushed him past his comfort zone. The smart thing would be to end their personal relationship here and now. They'd both slipped up—him more than her. No reason to compound the mistakes by persisting with their sexual relationship. Yet he couldn't bring himself to say goodbye.

"Teresa St. Claire offered me a job with her company," she said into the silence between them.

He wasn't surprised someone else had tried to snap her up. "Do you want to take it?"

Shane could see where the event planning business

would be a good fit for Isabel. And if she no longer worked for Richmond, he could pursue her without either of their careers being affected. This simple solution should've brought an end to his concern. Instead, it highlighted a new issue.

Was he ready for his life to change if he continued to date Isabel?

"I'm not sure," she said, her gaze shifting away. "It might be time to try something new. And it would be a lot less complicated…for us."

Her hesitation was a plea for him to reassure her that he was interested in something that extended past these next few days. As strongly as he believed in Isabel's talent and abilities, Shane couldn't honestly say if he'd been motivated to offer her a job at corporate so he'd have an excuse to stop seeing her. It might have been bad form to date a lowly concierge at one of his hotels, but they could've kept that under wraps. Promoting her into the Seattle office put extreme pressure on their relationship.

"Let's get through the Richmond retreat," he said. "We can discuss this more on the other side."

Disappointment chased across Isabel's features before she nodded. "Sure. Of course."

With his entire body alive with energy and lust, Liam forced himself to exit the massage room. Grappling with the painful act of turning his back on the woman he'd left spent and lethargic in the aftermath of her stunning orgasm, he marched toward the locker room, where he'd left his clothes. Teeth clenched against the pounding, urgent longing to return and take back his bitter rejection, Liam's hands shook as he changed into gray slacks and a black sweater before striding out of the spa without a backward glance.

Any relaxation he might've gained from the massage vanished in the aftermath of what had followed. Now, his jacked-up pulse sent waves of heat surging through his veins. His skin burned. Adrenaline whipped his nerve endings into a frenzy. He couldn't bear to head up to his empty suite and face the long night alone. Instead, he bypassed the bank of elevators, ignored the siren call of the bar's excellent selection of scotch and headed straight out the lobby doors into the night.

Rain-drenched wind lashed at his face but didn't slow him down. Distantly Liam noted the valet asking if he wanted his car, and he shook his head a second before stepping from beneath the entrance canopy into the downpour. Icy sheets of cold water struck him, plastering his hair to his head, penetrating the cotton fibers of his sweater and instantly banishing all heat from his skin. But even as his core temperature dipped, the rain did little to eliminate his emotional uproar.

What the hell had he just done? He promised himself he would not go there again. But all she had to do was crook a finger at him and he was on his knees, worshipping her.

Damn it.

What made it so much worse was that he wanted to do it all over again. And then to take her up on her offer to do the same to him. Just the thought of her mouth on him made his blood run wild and hot.

Half-blinded by the downpour, Liam headed away

from the hotel, following a sign that indicated the trail to the falls lay ahead. Calling himself all sorts of idiot, Liam strode onto the path, fighting the urge to shout curses at the top of his lungs. With the wind at his back, hastening him along, he reached the overlook at the top of the falls. Palms flat atop the stone wall, the thunder of the falls a concussive roar filling his ears, Liam lifted his voice in a series of savage curses at the woman who'd wronged his family and at himself for his inability to resist her.

The rain eased as his turmoil bled away. With each drop that struck him, he grew calmer and awakened to his foolishness. In fact, by the time he retraced his steps, he wished he'd never ventured out into the rain. Chilled and shivering, he reflected that a better response to the encounter with Teresa might have been to sit in the bar beside a roaring fire, sip an excellent twenty-five-year-old scotch or manhattan and size up various single women he'd noted days earlier.

Unfortunately, he couldn't summon the enthusiasm for a night of uncomplicated sex with a beautiful stranger. Since meeting Teresa, his focus had narrowed to one woman. One scheming, lying female who haunted him day and night.

Liam retreated back down the trail, feeling like an idiot as he entered the hotel through a side door, avoiding the lobby. Reluctant to have to explain his sodden clothes to anyone, he found the stairwell and jogged up the five flights of stairs. The exercise warmed him after the chill of outdoors. Relieved to have encountered no one, he opened the door his suite and stepped inside.

After shedding his sopping clothes on the bathroom floor, he stepped into the shower and turned the taps to blazing hot, and in moments the chill had left his skin. Dressed in gray slacks and a black crew neck sweater, he exited the suite once more. This time, when he approached the lobby, he wrapped himself in cool disdain and headed to the bar for a late dinner and a much-needed drink.

He was perusing the bar menu when a beautiful brunette approached his table.

"Hello, you're Liam Christopher, right?"

"Yes." He surveyed her slender figure, admiring the shapely legs bared by her figure-hugging black dress and made to look even longer by the stiletto heels she wore. A detached part of Liam appreciated the sexy beauty while wishing he could summon the enthusiasm to pursue her. "I'm sorry, you look familiar…"

She flashed an engaging grin. "Nicolette Ryan." She put out her hand and he automatically took it. "I do lifestyle reporting. I'm here to cover the Richmond retreat, where I understand your company is making a big announcement."

"Of course." Memory triggered, he recalled Matt telling him that she was invited because she knew how to respect a guest's privacy if they didn't want to be interviewed or shown on camera. "Would you like to join me for a drink?"

"Actually…" Her gaze strayed toward the bar's entrance. "I'm waiting for someone. But I'd love to sit down with you tomorrow if you have time."

He pulled up his calendar. Most of the day was booked. "How about four o'clock?"

Her high-wattage smile was intended to make him feel like the most important person in the room. "That would be perfect."

The heat he should've been feeling at being the focus of such a beautiful woman's attention never manifested. Instead, movement near the bar's entrance caught his notice. He glanced over in time to catch Teresa's entrance.

His mouth went dry.

Like Nicolette, she wore a snug black dress with lace-covered cutouts that enhanced her sex appeal. Her long blond hair cascaded in a silky curtain over one shoulder. Her composure didn't slip at all as she spied him speaking with Nicolette. In fact, her gaze swept past him and lingered on the reporter. Nicolette noticed his attention had wandered and glanced over her shoulder. Something passed between the two women before Nicolette gave a quick nod and turned back to Liam.

"I'll leave you to enjoy the rest of your evening," she said. "See you tomorrow at four."

And then she headed over to join Teresa at a quiet table in the back, leaving Liam to wonder what the two women could possibly have to discuss.

Twelve

With the Richmond retreat set to receive its first official guests the next day, Isabel and Shane stole away to her cabin for a late dinner. Something had changed between them since the night of their big talk. Although Shane had become Isabel's dream lover, when he wasn't making love to her with tenderness or raw passion, she found herself dreading the moment when he dropped the bomb, ending their fling.

Maybe that's why she devoted so much of their time together to getting him naked and ravishing him. It was easy to pretend she was in a perfect relationship while passion consumed them.

"Hear that?" Isabel asked, leaning over Shane's shoulder as he fed fresh logs onto the fire. She caressed his ear with her lips in the way she'd learned drove him crazy.

"What?"

"The wind has really picked up." Its howling stirred her blood, making her feel wild and untamed.

Shane got to his feet and glanced at the window. "Maybe I should head back to Seattle."

"Or…" She drew him toward the couch and gave him a firm shove. He dropped into the cushions with a startled grunt.

"Or?"

"You could spend the night here." As she spoke, she hiked up her full skirt and straddled his lap, letting her heat and the wetness that had slicked her panties drive his arousal hard. She curved her hands over his shoulders, savoring the power in his muscles.

His dark eyes heated as he curved his long fingers over her butt. "Are you sure you're not getting sick of me?" He bucked his hips upward, driving himself into her.

With a lazy smile she rode the motion, giving her hips a little grinding twist that earned her a hoarse moan. She loved that sound and didn't want to face never hearing it again.

"I like having you around, but if you think we're spending too much time together…" She made as if to get up. "I'll get your coat."

Before she could do more than shift her weight, his fingers bit into her hips, keeping her right where she was.

"Don't bother," he said, his voice husky. "I like being here with you."

"But how should we spend our time?" she purred, raking her nails through his hair.

"We could play a game."

The wind gusted, slapping rain against the windows. The whole cabin seemed to shudder at the impact. Or maybe that was just the storm surge of despair battering her heart as she realized that with the Richmond retreat starting tomorrow, this might be their last night together.

She rocked her hips, grinding herself against him. "What sort of a game?"

"I'm thinking of a number between one and ten. If you get it wrong, you take something off."

"I like this game." And the fact that he grew playful in her company. She leaned down and blew in his ear. "Four."

"Nope, sorry. The number was five."

"Damn," she murmured, shivering as he stripped her T-shirt over her head. Her nipples pebbled as his fingers grazed over her lace-covered breasts. "Your turn. Guess a number."

"Three."

"Nope, sorry," she said. "The number was seven."

She stripped off his dress shirt and hummed in appreciation as she trailed her palms over the smooth flesh of his shoulders and chest.

"Two," she crowed, his startled expression making her laugh. "What?"

"How'd you know that was the number I was thinking of?"

"First of all…" She pointed to her breasts. "And second, you do realize the point of this game is all about getting us naked, right?"

"Yes." He drew the word out, obviously not getting her point.

She grinned. "It's okay to cheat."

"Right," he murmured. "The number was five. You guessed wrong."

"Again?" She reached behind her and popped the clasp on her bra. "I guess this needs to go."

She tossed her lingerie aside and gave her head a vigorous shake, sending her hair spilling over her shoulder and setting her breasts to jiggling enticingly.

"You are gorgeous," Shane muttered, his voice hoarse with desire. He gathered her breasts into his hands. "These are gorgeous."

Smiling in appreciation, she gave her hips another rocking twist and heard a rush of air through his parted lips. She liked that it was easy to turn him on. Her confidence bloomed still more as he cursed before dipping his head to capture one nipple in his mouth. As his tongue worked over the hard bud, he curved his hands over her hips, fingers biting into her flesh while she worked a sexy bump and grind on him.

Leaning forward, she rubbed her cheek against his stubble, enjoying the sandpaper feel of it against her skin. It was a stark contrast to the softness of his wavy black hair that caressed her fingers as she drove them through the silky waves. Her senses awakened to his every micromovement. The bunch of his leg muscles against her inner thighs. The subtle hitch in his breath beneath the rumbling encouragement pouring from his throat. The dip of his lashes as he tried to read her.

"Kiss me," he said, his tone as much request as demand.

"My pleasure."

She crushed her lips to his, drinking in his low moan of satisfaction. The hard kiss told him she intended to own the moment. Her fingers curved around his head, as she parted her lips and sent her tongue questing forward. She'd never been interested in stuff like this with other guys she dated. Mostly because they'd been more interested in their pleasure than hers.

In contrast, Shane gave and gave and gave before he took his own pleasure. Having a man hanging on your every moan was incredibly sexy. The other way he'd surprised her was how he was okay with her taking the lead from time to time. With someone who liked control as much as Shane, she'd expected he would prefer to be in charge all the time. Instead, she'd discovered that her aggressiveness turned him on.

Which was good for her and better for him. She liked him fully aroused. Insanely hungry. Mad with anticipation. And tonight, she intended to blow his mind.

Isabel broke off the kiss. "It's your turn. Pick a number," she panted, kissing her way down his chest. Her hand had already trailed over his abs and made its way south of his belt.

"Sex!" The word shot out of him as she molded her fingers over the hard length of him pushing against his zipper. "Six." He cursed. And then laughed.

"Wrong," she crowed, shifting off his lap in order to get at his pants.

"Where are you going?" He sounded half-desperate and that made her smile.

"I'm not going anywhere." She made quick work of his belt and zipper. "But these are."

Once he was down to his boxers, she stood and set her hands on her hips, taking him in while giving him time to ogle her lean, fit body. She'd worked hard to earn all the muscles on display and was gratified to see approval in his eyes. His anticipatory grin made her greedy for more.

Even as his eyes grew hot and his erection tented his boxers, she became aware of an equally insistent pulse between her thighs. She wanted him. Inside her. Driving hard and fast toward his climax. Taking her with him. Making her pant and moan and even scream. She caught her lips between her teeth as a growl of pleasure rattled out of him.

"The underwear next," he said, his raspy tone and greedy gaze driving her pleasure higher. "I want to see all of you."

She liked being told by Shane what to do during sex. That he shared his needs with her, described what felt good, what turned him on. All this gave their lovemaking an unexpected intimacy. For a man who kept his cards close to his chest, she knew more about him than she'd ever dreamed.

"What else do you want?" she asked him, turning and sliding her panties off one hip and then the other. She glanced back at him and, seeing she had his full attention, bent forward at the waist to slide her underwear down her legs.

His curse left her smiling. To further drive him crazy, she caressed her fingertips up her thighs and over the curves of her butt, imagining how she'd feel when Shane's hands made the same journey.

"You have a spectacular ass, did you know that?"

"What? This old thing?" Straightening, she gave herself a little spank before turning around. "I've had it forever."

"I wouldn't mind having it forever," he said, holding out his hand. "A man could die happy with such a beautiful thing in his life."

Isabel didn't know what to make of his words, so she decided not to think too much. She planned to imprint every second of their time together in her mind. He was a man worth remembering long after their paths diverged.

"I don't think you need these any longer." With a sassy smile, she leaned forward and hooked her fingers into the waistband of his boxers. Her sharp downward yank made him grunt in surprise, but a moment later he was grinning.

As his erection appeared, she licked her lips in anticipation. The heavy pulse between her thighs thundered mercilessly as she knelt between his long legs. Plying him with hands and mouth, she intended to drive him crazy, and then leave him shattered and spent.

"Isabel?"

She dipped her head and flicked him with her tongue, smiling at the raw expletive that tore loose from him.

"Like that?" she teased, going back for a second, longer lick.

A husky groan rattled free as he slouched back and gave himself completely over to her ministrations. Yet as relaxed and open as he appeared, his sable eyes remained a bit wary.

"I want this to be good for you," she said. "Let me."

She wrapped her hand around the base of his shaft and slowly settled her mouth over him. He tasted salty and sexy and a wildness spread through her blood. The low sounds of pleasure rattling in his chest boosted her confidence and Isabel glanced at his face.

He'd closed his eyes and was breathing hard. Concentration mingled with awe suffused his expression. His fingers were clenched in a death grip on a throw pillow and Isabel realized now was the time to turn up the heat. She worked her mouth over him, combining tantalizing swirls of her tongue with coordinated movements of her lips and hand.

"You're killing me," he muttered as she took him as deep as possible.

She answered by increasing the pace just enough to make him moan her name, and then his fingers threaded through her hair, guiding her head.

He exhaled raggedly. "Feels amazing."

Isabel had more surprises up her sleeve and shifted her free hand to cup his balls. His body jerked in surprise at her light squeeze and his fingers tightened on her scalp. A moment later, whereas up until now he'd been still and nearly docile beneath her, he began lifting his hips and rocking forward into her.

From the sounds he was making and the near agony of his expression, Isabel knew what he needed. And wanted to give him a moment he'd never forget. So, she gave him her mouth and made herself a willing receptacle for his pleasure.

As he realized what she'd offered, his eyes went wide. She met his gaze and offered him a wicked half smile. A second later he shuddered and began thrusting. The power of his joy intensified her own pleasure and she raked her nails across his skin. The minor pain acted like a torch, setting him on fire.

His thighs began to tremble. His body quaked. No shout or loud groan accompanied his orgasm. In fact, she thought he stopped breathing as he came.

In the aftermath, she sat back on her heels and grinned. "Okay?"

He cracked his eyes open. "Okay?" A weak chuckle sounded. "Hell, no. I'm not okay. You've ruined me."

His reaction was all she could hope for and more. "Sorry."

"You aren't one bit sorry." Shane reached down and hauled her up and forward until she lay sprawled across his naked body. His fingers cupped her cheek. "You loved that and I loved that."

She went all shivery inside at his use of the word *loved*. Something rattled loose in her chest. As much as she'd tried to protect herself from being hurt by staying focused on the red-hot sex between them, Isabel conceded she'd already lost that battle. Dozens of times a day the *L*-word leaped into the front of her mind. It had become as relentless as the downpour outside.

"And you trusted me," he continued. "Let me do it hard." He brought his lips to hers and it was a reverent kiss. "Thank you." A pause. "For the trust."

She tensed a little as he brought up the tricky subject. While it was true that she trusted him with her body, believed he'd treat her carefully, what remained undefined between them gave her frequent anxious moments.

Burying her face in the spot where his shoulder and neck came together, Isabel murmured, "Of course I trust you."

Normally the view out the main ballroom's twenty-foot wall of windows was nothing short of spectacular. Today, driving rain obscured the manicured lawn and the pine-covered mountains far beyond. At the edge of the stone terrace that ran alongside the building, wind hammered tall, ancient trees. Their branches whipped back and forth with each gust.

The storm mirrored the turmoil Teresa felt inside. It wasn't just the looming party that was agitating her or the problems presented by the storm, but what had happened between her and Liam at the spa. She was still kicking herself for going there with him again. Why couldn't she just accept that they were done? In the coming months she would be sitting on Christopher Corporation's board and she needed to start treating him like a professional colleague.

Yet she couldn't shake that after what had happened between them in the spa, all her hastily built defenses were little more than scattered piles of rubble. Nor could she blame Liam for the destruction. After all, she'd handed him the sledgehammer. How did she proceed with him going forward? Fantastic sex wasn't going to fix what was broken between them no matter how often they gave it their all. The reality was that he didn't trust her. Or couldn't. No, in fact, he didn't want to.

Teresa peered past the rain pounding the ballroom's windows, gaze tracing the curving paths that criss-crossed the lawn while she assessed the planting beds that bordered them. Would anything be left of the lush foliage after this storm had passed? As she watched, a lounge cushion tumbled past on its way toward the river and the one-hundred-thirty-foot drop.

With the storm intensifying, flooding and wind damage threatened the party preparations. Florists were supposed to be arriving from Seattle today with truckloads of stunning arrangements to fill every suite in The Opulence. Navigating the winding roads in this sort of weather would be treacherous. What if they refused to make the journey? Or couldn't?

Teresa grimaced. She had to stop focusing on what-ifs and maybes.

So what if she didn't have flowers? She had the well-stocked welcome baskets to distract them as well as the incredible gift bags each retreat attendee received. At least she'd made sure those items arrived early. Her staff was delivering the baskets even now and making sure each suite was personalized to the attendee.

The sheer rage of the storm drew Teresa closer to the glass. She couldn't believe the violence of the wind and rain. She'd never seen anything like it in the Pacific Northwest. It was unusual. More than unusual—it was once in a lifetime. She shivered. If this kept up, the party was going to be…

Even as her mind went there, something large moved outside. A dark shape began toppling toward her. Buffeted by the wind, one of the oak trees at the edge of the terrace had given up its battle. The volume of rain they'd received over the last week combined with the violent winds had loosened the roots in the ground. It was falling. Teresa watched it come down in slow motion. It didn't occur to her to step back until she could identify the individual leaves shivering as they advanced.

Her mind started shrieking at her. *Run!* As Teresa turn to flee, the lights went out. Disoriented, her heel snagged on the carpet and a red-hot spike ripped through her ankle. Her head clipped the back of a chair as she fell to her knees. Dizzy, she heard the sound of shattering glass behind her. The storm roared like a beast freed and a hard blow landed on her shoulder from behind. Icy water drenched her as the heavy weight drove her to the ground and trapped her beneath its wet, leafy mass.

Liam was having a drink in the bar with Nicolette Ryan when he heard a distant boom and noticed several hotel employees racing through the lobby. The lights blinked out, but within twenty seconds the backup generator clicked on. Never one to sit by when something was going wrong, he excused himself to the reporter, jumped to his feet and followed.

"A tree crashed through the ballroom's windows and a woman's trapped," a man in a gray shirt and pants called as he passed Liam. "We'll need a chainsaw to get her out."

"Does anybody know who's trapped?" Liam asked as he moved through the crowd that had gathered to view the devastation.

"Teresa St. Claire was meeting with Aspen here a few minutes ago," one of the waitstaff said. "It might be either one of them."

Liam bolted across the room toward a familiar blond head half-hidden by the autumn-brown leaves of one of the ancient oaks. Nearly a third of the tree had crashed through the wall of windows. Heedless of the rain-soaked carpet, Liam dropped to one knee beside Teresa, appalled that she didn't seem to be moving. The roaring storm hadn't let up at all and the voices behind and around him faded as he reached for her.

The wind blew water into his eyes as Liam touched her cheek, feeling the chill beneath his fingers. *She can't be dead. Don't let her be dead.* Even as these thoughts chased through his head, she gave a slight moan and her lashes fluttered. Liam didn't realize how afraid he'd been until his heart gave a huge bump against his breastbone.

"Teresa. Teresa, can you hear me?"

"What...?"

Her fingers dug into the carpet like she was trying to crawl out from beneath the weight bearing down on her. He grabbed the branch pinning her to the ground and applied all this strength, but couldn't budge it. There was nothing for him to do but wait for reinforcements and the helplessness ate at him.

"Don't try to move," Liam told her. "You have a tree on top of you."

"A tree?" She blinked and that seemed to clear her thoughts. Fear widened her eyes.

Frustrated, Liam glanced around and noted all the people standing around, including Nicolette Ryan, who'd followed him from the bar. As much as he wanted to scream at them to do something, keeping Teresa calm was his first priority.

"We're working to get you out. Maintenance is coming with a chainsaw. Hang in there."

It was the most agonizing ten minutes of his life as he waited for the guy to return. When he did, the maintenance man came with reinforcements and Liam was grateful that The Opulence operated with such smooth efficiency. Working together, the men had the limb cut and Teresa freed in short order. She shifted into a sitting position and picked dead leaves from her clothes as Liam knelt beside her.

"Are you okay?" He stroked her damp hair away from her face and surveyed her features.

"My shoulder is sore." She shifted her feet under her, preparing to rise, and winced, grabbing at her left ankle. "And I think I might've twisted my ankle as I tried to get out of the way."

Liam didn't wait for her to say another word. He carefully lifted her into his arms and carried her out of the ballroom, conscious that his dramatic gesture was drawing everyone's attention. Including the reporter, who had her cell phone up and a pleased smile on her face as she watched him walk past.

It might be ridiculous to feel so protective about a woman he claimed that he was done with. If she hadn't been hurt he might've been able to keep that promise. Seeing her lying beneath that tree had made him realize that she still got to him, but he had no idea how to move past all the doubts and recriminations.

He carried her into his suite and set her down on the couch. "I'll get you some ice." He found a plastic bag in one of the kitchenette drawers and poured ice into it.

She winced as he applied the cold bag to her ankle. "Thanks."

"You should get out of those wet clothes."

Despite her obvious pain and although she still looked shaken by her ordeal, one slim eyebrow rose in a mocking salute. Realizing how she'd taken what he'd meant as a practical suggestion, he frowned.

"I can find something of mine for you to wear." He suddenly noticed his own damp clothing. "I think we both need to get dry."

"You could just take me back to my room," she said, but didn't sound as if she wanted to go.

"I think someone should keep an eye on you."

She gave him a sad smile. "And you're volunteering?"

"I'll get you some dry clothes."

When he returned, she was reviewing the contract his lawyer had sent over for Liam to review. It had been sitting on the coffee table. She wore a frown as she scanned the document. As he dropped a T-shirt and his pajama bottoms beside her, Teresa glanced up.

"Why is it so hard for you to trust?"

"I grew up believing that I shouldn't give anyone the benefit of the doubt."

"Why?"

"My mother has always been convinced that people were out to get her, and she had plenty of examples that proved it." While he'd offered a straightforward answer to her direct question, admitting such a profound failing about someone he loved felt like the bitterest betrayal.

"I didn't know her that well, but she was nothing but polite to me. Even when she thought I was sleeping with her husband."

"She's very good at making her fears seem rational. Maybe if she raved about conspiracies it would've been easier to dismiss her claims." For several seconds Liam closed his eyes. "It got worse after she and my father divorced. Over and over she urged me to question whether my friends had my back. But even when it was obvious they did, a tiny voice in the back of my mind always doubted."

"I get it," Teresa said. "While I couldn't do what I do without my team, I'm always checking up on them, rarely giving them the freedom to do their job without being second-guessed by me."

"It drove my dad crazy. That's why he divorced my mom."

"Do you think it will always get in the way of us…?" She faltered and stared at the contract in her hands. "Of us working together?"

Liam didn't think she'd started out asking about their professional relationship.

"When it comes to business, I've hired the best people and trust them to do what needs to be done. I take steps to make sure I know all the information I need before making a decision. It's my personal life I struggle with." Especially in light of the way Teresa was keeping the truth from him regarding her relationship with his father. "How do I know if I can fall in love and not be hurt?"

"How do any of us know?" Teresa set aside the document. "I guess we're a pair. Like you, I've wrapped myself up in growing my business because it's safe and use work as an excuse for why I don't date. But the truth is, you're the first man I've wanted to be with in a long, long time."

"I want to be with you, as well," Liam said, surprising himself with the admission. "I just don't know how to get past everything that's between us."

Teresa nodded. "Neither do I."

Thirteen

Gasping for breath, Isabel fell onto her back, too spent to lift her arm and clear the strand of hair away from her sweat-soaked skin.

"Damn, you're good at that," she murmured. "I don't think I'll ever be able to move again."

Shane chuckled…*chuckled*…as he headed into the bathroom to dispose of the condom. Lots and lots of sex obviously agreed with him. Everyone at the hotel had been commenting on how relaxed he looked despite all the problems brought on by the days of rain and high winds. And every time one of her coworkers wondered why he looked so happy, Isabel had to hide a smile.

No one knew they'd been sneaking around. They'd been very careful to keep their interaction at the hotel to a minimum and when they did speak, neither one of them behaved in anything less than a professional manner. For Isabel's part, she knew how much Shane valued his reputation. Nor did she want anyone to view his offer of promotion as anything other than something she'd earned because of the solid work she'd done for the hotel.

Isabel grinned at the joy humming through her. She had a lot to be happy about at the moment. Great sex with Shane. Her career taking off. But the bulk of her pleasure came from the transformation of this logical workaholic into a man driven by his passionate need for her and his willingness to open up about things he'd long kept bottled up.

A string of curses flew through the open bathroom door, each one more biting than the last, and intruded on her blissful glow. Isabel lifted onto her elbows and stared toward the source of the sounds.

"What's wrong?" she asked, imagining all sorts of issues that could've come up given the way the rain lashed at the windows.

Shane appeared in the doorway. Backlit by the bathroom's light, his face in shadow, the power of his naked body took her breath away. She'd traced his chiseled muscles with her fingertips and lips. Felt the impact of his lean strength as he pressed her into the mattress. Such tactile experiences had been amazing, but she could spend the rest of her life staring at his broad shoulders, lean hips and corded muscles without ever growing tired of the sight.

"The condom had a tear," he growled, raking his fingers through his hair, the gesture reflecting acute worry and annoyance. "Damn it. This can't be happening."

"Oh." She absorbed this information and ran it through a series of filters. While the development wasn't great, it wasn't exactly dire. First off was the issue of safety. She hadn't had a lot of partners and was always very careful and assumed Shane was, as well. "We should be okay."

"Okay?" he demanded. Advancing toward the bed, he clicked on the bedside light. "It's not okay. The condom broke. That's a problem."

"You don't have to worry about catching anything from me," she explained, rushing to reassure him.

"I'm not worried about catching anything," he said, his brown eyes cold and distant as he gazed at her. "I'm worried about getting you pregnant."

"You don't need to be." Before she could elaborate that she was on the pill because of her irregular periods, Shane started grabbing up his clothes and putting them on.

"There's a morning-after pill or something, isn't there? Do you need a prescription or is it something you can get over the counter? Is there a drugstore nearby that's open at this hour?"

He was so busy peppering her with questions while he dressed that he hadn't yet noticed she was frowning at him. She'd never seen him so distraught. He was positively frantic.

"Let me look up some information on that." He grabbed his phone and began tapping away. "Okay, it says here that you can get it over the counter." He glanced at the window as a gust of wind threw rain against the glass. "Damn it. We probably shouldn't go anywhere in this." He glanced back down at his phone. "Maybe we'll be okay." Shane's breath gusted out as the last bit of information calmed him down somewhat. "If this information is correct, it's ninety-five percent effective if you take it within 24 hours."

If his blind panic hadn't felt a lot like stinging rejection, Isabel might've found the whole thing amusing. But she was falling in love with this man, and his horror over her potential pregnancy had been authentic and intense. This eye-opening glimpse of him was completely at odds with the solid, dependable man she'd come to know, and ice settled into her bones at the mistake she'd made in opening herself up to him.

Which was probably why she didn't resist the need to strike back.

"If you're so paranoid about getting a woman pregnant, perhaps you should check the expiration date on your condoms." Her voice shook as she vented her humiliation and grief. "And while you're at it, maybe stock up on the morning-after pill so if things like this happen in the future, you'll be able to eliminate the threat before it has a chance to become a problem."

His gaze whipped to her, and Isabel immediately regretted her words and tone. Of course he was worried about the future havoc a broken condom could have on his life. Had he not spent enough time warning her that his focus was solely on his career? He didn't want to make time for a relationship, much less a child.

"Isabel…"

Heart breaking, she flung up both her hands. "Oh, please don't."

And then, to her profound relief, his phone began to ring.

* * *

"I can't…" Shane began, unsure how to proceed.

He couldn't what? Offer her a future? Handle more than a few blissful days of great sex? He'd done what he'd sworn to avoid and let himself get tangled up in her. They'd never discussed where things went beyond these few days. The fact remained that she was his employee. A valuable one. He didn't want to lose her. In business. Or in his personal life. The fact that he'd put himself in a place where he would be forced to choose inspired a string of condemnations to run through his mind.

"This is all going really fast," he continued. "I don't know how you fit in my life."

The devastated expression on Isabel's face was like a knife through Shane's heart. Damn it. He'd never promised her anything, but from what she'd said, it was obvious that he'd mishandled the situation. Explaining to her that he'd only been concerned for her welfare would fly as well as a plane without wings. He hadn't once asked her if she was okay or even let her join him in being anxious.

Instead, she'd sat as cool and composed as always and watched him fall apart.

Now she glanced at his ringing phone. "I think you'd better answer that call. If someone is trying to get ahold of you at this hour, it must be important."

Stomach twisted in knots, he accepted the call. "What?"

At first there was silence on the line and then a man spoke. "It's Benny Jacobs. I'm with maintenance at The Opulence." He sounded worried and more than a little nervous.

Rubbing the back of his neck, Shane tempered his tone. "Sure, Benny. What can I do for you?"

"There's a problem here at the hotel. A big one. And we can't get ahold of Tom Busch."

"What happened?" Shane asked, startled to find that for the first time in his life, he wanted to avoid a work-related crisis.

His gaze followed Isabel as she got out of bed and started pulling on jeans and a long-sleeved blouse. Her motions were jerky and her features wore a hard, determined look he'd never seen before. The implications created a ball of dread in his gut.

"One of those old trees fell and punched a big hole in the main ballroom." Benny went on to explain how they were handling things. "The storm has the guests pretty stirred up."

"I'll be there as soon as I can." He hung up the phone and turned to Isabel. "I have to go back to the hotel." He quickly explained the situation.

"I'm coming with you. If the guests are upset, the more staff on hand, the better."

"Thanks." Grateful for her help, Shane headed out of the bedroom. He paused just outside the doorway. "And later we should talk."

"Let's just worry about the guests for now."

That he'd made a mess of things was abundantly clear as they raced out to his car. Nor did he get any time to figure out what to say to make things better. The three-mile drive back to the hotel should've taken less than ten minutes, but with downed branches littering the road and the heavy winds blowing blinding rain and debris at them, visibility had diminished so he could barely see three feet ahead of his front bumper. Shane was forced to creep along lest he hit something or miss a place where the road had washed out.

Deciding to take only his vehicle might have been a blessing or a curse. Granted, it was one fewer car on the road, but the only time Isabel spoke during the half-hour trip was to warn him of obstacles in their path. After a disagreement like they'd had, another woman might've taken the enforced proximity to hammer at him with her anger. Isabel was unique. She'd obviously set aside her unhappiness in order to cope with the current crisis. This allowed Shane the space he needed to focus on the road and made him admire her all the more.

She was a romantic idealist, filled with fantastic plans for how to make people happy. Her eloquent passion had touched his cold, dead heart, bringing him to life like a magical kiss from a princess. Was it any wonder that her favorite animated movie was *Beauty and the Beast?* With him cast as the beast to her beauty?

Yet the joy she'd brought into his life hadn't completely transformed him. When duty called, he was happy to turn his back on a woman who'd needed to be reassured of his strong feelings for her. He'd prioritized his career over his personal life so many times that it was second nature. It was safe.

Putting out fires. Fixing problems. Maximizing potential. All these things were activities within his control. They required order and logic. And filled him with satisfaction.

Or they had until he'd let himself be charmed by Isabel's smiles and fanciful ideas of love and romance.

Seeing her smile. Hearing her cry out in passion. Losing himself in her heat. With her he felt invincible and more vulnerable than he ever had. He'd placed the power to tear him apart into her soft, tender hands, and then, like a stubborn fool, he'd snatched it back. No doubt she forgave him for playing games with her, understanding that his behavior was based in fear.

Before she got out of the car she turned to him. "What are we doing?" Even before she finished the question, she was shaking her head. "Never mind," she said, disappointment making her brisk as she fumbled for the door handle. "Forget I asked."

But her velvety hazel eyes begged him to tell her what she meant to him.

He wanted to be honest with her, but fell back on tired platitudes instead. "I never think about my future in terms of a relationship."

That wasn't what he meant to say—not at all. But the thought of her pregnant left him confronting the possibility that he could be a dad. The panic returned, twisting him up and rendering him frozen and searching for answers. What if he didn't have the temperament for parenthood? He sure as hell didn't have a good role model to draw inspiration from.

His instincts told him to rely on Isabel. She'd drawn him to the edge of a cliff, shown him a world of adventure and delight waiting for him to explore. He only had to take a risk and follow her past his comfort zone. Let himself walk beside her into the unknown.

But instead of trusting her to help him, Shane stumbled back.

Gutless bastard.

She deserved to know how she made him feel. Confused. Enthusiastic. Ravenous. All things foreign to a man who ruled his emotions with iron control.

But he wasn't an adventurer, someone who reached for the stars while balanced on the top rung of a wobbly ladder, one step above the sign that warned: This Is Not a Step. Which was exactly why he needed her to inspire him to take risks so he could feel alive.

"I'm sorry. I shouldn't have asked. I told myself not to put you on the spot." Isabel gave a funny, awkward laugh. "It's the weather. All the wind and rain. It has everyone stirred up."

"It's not the weather," he growled.

Although he didn't deserve it, she put her free hand against his cheek and gave him a heartbreaking smile of sympathy and acceptance. "It's okay. Really. I'm a die-hard romantic. I see happy endings for everyone. It's a curse."

"It's a gift," he countered, his tone brooking no argument. He recognized that she often regressed into self-mockery to ease a tense situation, but he couldn't allow her to downplay her greatest strength. "You're a gift."

Her eyes widened at his husky declaration and her throat worked. "Thank you."

And then she was throwing open the car door and flinging herself into the rain-drenched night, leaving their single umbrella behind for him. Thoughts a tumultuous mess, Shane watched her hunched figure disappear through the lobby doors.

What if she was pregnant?

Such a thing would cause his entire life to unravel.

Children deserved green space to run and play, so he'd have to move out of his bachelor pad in downtown Seattle and find a house in the suburbs with a yard and a longer commute because he'd chosen a neighborhood with the best schools. He'd buy a sensible car based on its good safety ratings.

His son or daughter would also demand more of his time, forcing him to rebalance his life, taking fewer business trips, spending less hours at the office, eating dinner at home.

But beyond the physical changes that would affect his home and career, something subtler would take place, as well. He'd no longer be focused on himself. Both Isabel and the child would become permanent fixtures in his world. Any decisions he made would be with them in mind.

In a sudden flash, Shane saw himself sitting on the floor while his child played with building blocks. He pictured himself getting up in the middle of the night to soothe a crying baby, letting Isabel catch up on some much-needed sleep. Side by side they would cheer at soccer games and clap enthusiastically at school plays, take prom photos and team up on game night.

How did he know this was how he'd behave? Because it was the exact opposite of what his father had done.

With his future spooling through his mind like a sentimental TV commercial, the grievances Shane had clung to fell away. He'd sacrificed his twenties to proving his father wrong, burying himself in work to advance his career. His friends had gotten married and started families and he'd drifted away from them, cynically believing that his choices were the right ones. Every promotion, every pay raise had demonstrated that he was the successful one. Never once had he questioned if that was true.

Enough.

The time had come to make some changes in his life. Starting with a certain free-spirited redhead who'd struck a spark and brought him to life.

Dimly aware that Teresa had left at some point before dawn to check on the ballroom's broken windows, Liam was brought to full wakefulness by the alarm on his phone around seven. He opened his eyes to face an empty suite and the realization that, based on the wild storm the night before and the damage to the hotel, it was pretty clear the Richmond retreat would have to be postponed. Due to her ankle, Teresa had spent the majority of the night on her phone, controlling the chaos from his suite, while Liam had talked to Matt several times, giving him hourly updates.

He had just finished a long hot shower when his phone rang. It was his private investigator.

"Hey," he said, tossing aside the towel he'd been using on his hair. "What's going on? Did you find anything out that connects Teresa and my father?"

"Nothing new. It doesn't seem as if they had any connection in the years between when your parents divorced and when you started seeing her."

Liam greeted this information with a mix of relief and frustration. "There has to be something. My dad wouldn't just give away twenty-five percent of his stock without a damn good reason."

"Well, there is one thing. Did you know that Teresa's father, Nigel St. Claire, worked for Christopher Corporation twenty years ago?"

This was news to Liam. "Doing what?" he asked, remembering that she'd lost her father when she was around six years old.

"He'd been active on some projects. I wasn't able to find out too much because of how spotty the records were from back then."

"And why is this just coming up now?"

"When I couldn't find anything about Teresa, I started looking at her parents."

"And you're sure it was Teresa's father?"

"Positive. He interned during college and then came on full-time once he graduated. There was a note in his file that he'd taken a leave of absence to deal with some family issues and never came back. Do you want me to dig further? See what sort of projects he was working on?"

Did he? A chill of premonition chased down Liam's spine that he quickly dispelled. Chances were his father hadn't known some low-level staffer. The whole thing was nothing more than a coincidence.

"See what you can find out," Liam said before hanging up with the PI.

Why hadn't Teresa ever mentioned that her father had worked for Christopher Corporation? Surely she'd known. Could this explain why his father had given her the stock?

Liam had just completed his packing when his phone rang a second time that morning.

"Tell me it isn't true," his mother demanded.

"Tell you what isn't true?" Liam countered, wishing he hadn't picked up the phone. "Do you know anything about Teresa's father working for Dad?"

His mother seemed confused by the question. "Why would I know anything about that?"

"I thought maybe that explained why Dad would've left her the shares."

"Your father made a fool of himself where that girl was concerned. And so are you." Catherine sounded aggrieved. "Oh, Liam, how could you?"

He decided not to play dumb. "My personal life is my business."

"And mine. What you do affects me." Her voice broke. "I can't have their affair coming up in public."

"There was no proof that they had an affair," Liam corrected her, annoyed that she kept bringing this up. He didn't want to confront his own doubts on the matter. "That was all a misunderstanding."

"And now you're sleeping with her, too."

"It's over."

"Not according to the story I'm reading."

"What story?" Gut twisting in dismay, he flashed back to the meeting between Teresa and Nicolette in the bar.

"And it's not just a story. There are pictures, as well."

Liam closed his eyes and counted to ten. "I'll look into it."

Fourteen

In the wake of the storm, Teresa navigated the chaotic lobby on the crutches the doctor had given her last night, dead smartphone clutched in her hand. People clustered in knots, buzzing about the damage in the aftermath of the storm, making plans to get away as soon as the roads cleared. So much had gone wrong. All her careful planning up in smoke.

Not even Jessie Humphrey at the piano, giving an impromptu concert, could fix what ailed her. As she hobbled past unhappy guests and stressed hotel staff, two things struck her at once. Foremost in her mind was the reality that she urgently needed a new venue for the Richmond retreat. Yet despite the blow to the event and potential damage to her career, she was happier than she'd been in weeks.

Liam had opened up to her in a way she'd never imagined possible following his anger at her for being included in Linus's will. That he'd shared his private concerns about his mother's behavior had touched Teresa's heart. The admission hadn't been easy for him to make and demonstrated that he might be able to move past his distrust of her. As to why that had such a disconcerting impact on her spirits, Teresa wasn't ready to scrutinize.

Approaching the concierge desk, Teresa held up her phone. "I've misplaced my charger. Do you have anywhere I can plug this in?"

Isabel gave her usual affirmative nod and held out her hand. As she plugged in Teresa's phone, the landline on the concierge desk began to ring. Showing no sign of her obvious fatigue from the previous night's wild weather, Isabel offered a bright greeting to the caller. After listening for several seconds, she caught Teresa's eye and mouthed the words *Matt Richmond*.

"Yes, it was a crazy evening," Isabel said. "But no one was seriously hurt, and Shane rallied the troops to get tarps in place over the damaged areas and has already spoken with the insurance adjusters."

When Teresa raised her eyebrows at how much information Isabel possessed regarding Shane's activities, a rosy color bloomed on the concierge's cheeks, but there was no sign of her usual happy smile.

"That's because her cell phone died at some point last night," Isabel explained. "She's standing right here. I can put her on." Isabel extended the phone to Teresa.

"Hello, Matt," Teresa began, bracing herself for the conversation to come.

"I've gathered from Liam and Shane's reports that things are under control, but still chaotic." The CEO sounded tense and on edge.

"Shane is on top of everything having to do with the property." Teresa glanced toward the front doors, where a woman was berating a valet for the dent her car sustained during the storm. Before things spiraled out of control, Shane arrived on the scene and calmed the woman within minutes. "And he's been smoothing things with the guests. Everyone is pretty upset."

"Obviously the party will have to be postponed."

"I'm afraid so. I've already started looking for a new venue." She didn't add that the first three places she'd contacted were booked solid for the next two months.

"I appreciate your quick response to the situation."

"Of course." After all, this party's success was going to give her company a major boost. "Do you have a date in mind for the retreat to be rescheduled?"

"Not at the moment. Perhaps we can schedule a meeting at my office to discuss it after you settle everything there."

"Sure. I was planning on heading back to Seattle tomorrow." Meanwhile she'd get Corrine to start a list of potential locations.

"I'm sorry I'm not there to deal with my guests. Nadia and I are still planning to arrive this morning," Matt said, surprising Teresa with the apology. "It was my party. You shouldn't have to bear the brunt of everyone's displeasure over how things turned out."

His concern touched her. "I appreciate that, but dealing with problems is part of what you hired me to do."

"Still, I want you to know that I understand the difficult position I put you in."

"Thank you." The conversation gave her hope that whatever challenges she faced next during her scramble to pull together a whole new event, he wouldn't judge her too harshly. "I'll let you know when I get back to Seattle. Hopefully I'll have a replacement venue by then."

She hung up the phone and glanced at her cell. Enough battery life had been replaced to wake the phone. Without unplugging it, she cued up her main screen and noticed she had a dozen missed calls. Surprised it wasn't more, Teresa checked to see who'd tried to get ahold of her.

Joshua had called her five times last night. Five! Teresa's heart contracted in fear. Nothing for weeks and now this sudden flurry of calls. That couldn't be good. She dialed his number and fumed when the call rolled to his voice mail. She left a brief explanation of the storm and told him to call her back. Then she went to the messages to see if he'd left her a voice mail, only to see he hadn't.

Panic and annoyance fought for domination as she wondered what had inspired his urgent attempts to get ahold of her. The last time she'd spoken with Joshua, he said he had everything under control. Guilt threaded through her anxiety. Her chest tightened, making breathing difficult. Joshua was her brother. Her responsibility. And now she couldn't reach him.

Teresa glanced at her phone, debating whether to

reach out to the Fixer again. She already owed him one favor. Could she afford two? She certainly couldn't ask Liam for help again. The battery indicator glowed red with warning. How much time did she have to deal with this new problem? She shivered, remembering her turmoil when she believed her brother had been kidnapped. That hoax reminded her to question everything about her brother's current situation.

That realization sparked a new revelation. Her cynicism gave her new insight into Liam's knee-jerk reactions. When the truth has been twisted over and over, how do you know what to believe? She'd only been dealing with Joshua's latest escapades for a few weeks. What would it be like to spend your entire life forced to sort out conflicting stories from people you loved and trusted?

As if her thoughts had drawn him to her, Teresa spied Liam striding in her direction. The shifting crowd filling the hotel lobby made his path irregular and offered Teresa ample time to survey his tall form. Her spirits executed a familiar somersault as their gazes met, but just as quickly she picked up on his tension and her skin prickled with uneasiness. She recognized that grim look, having seen it all too often in the last several weeks.

"We have to talk," he said, tension compressing his tone into a growl.

Isabel barely noticed when the wind and rain stopped around dawn. Operating by the glow of the emergency lights, she'd spent the night making herself useful wherever she could from dealing with the guests who'd come to the front desk demanding to know when the power was going to come back on, to pitching in with room-to-room checks to make sure people were okay.

Later, she and Aspen had huddled in a corner of the ballroom and stared at the devastation as the maintenance guys did their best to remove the tree and tack tarps over the massive hole. In her friend's eyes, Isabel glimpsed the grim reality that months and months of events would have to be canceled. All Aspen's hard work and planning plus the stress for the brides who could no longer look forward to their dream weddings at the hotel as well as the revenue the hotel would lose from corporate events.

Through the night and into the morning, while Isabel worked, her thoughts were never far from Shane. The last week had been a whirlwind. She'd never imagined Shane would be so good for her career or her personal life. He made her happier than she'd ever known. She'd fallen in love with him despite his being a stubborn, disciplined realist. In fact, it was his inflexibility and tunnel vision when it came to work that proved just how much he needed her.

But now that she'd glimpsed his sharp resistance to the things she wanted for her future, could she stay with him? Should she? Her heart told her he could change his mind. In less than two weeks he'd already become a less controlled, more lighthearted version of himself. Was it possible he could fully transform into the man she'd glimpsed over the last few days? The one who communicated and was considerate of her needs. Who smiled more and bent the rules.

Yet Teresa's warning about Shane had planted a seed that sent deep roots of doubt into her soul. In the aftermath of how he reacted when the condom broke, could she ever fully trust that he wouldn't wake up one day and regret that their time together had distracted him from what he believed was important?

Isabel recognized that it wasn't like her to go dark when so many things about life filled her with joy and enthusiasm, but had she ever been out on a ledge as far as she let herself go with Shane Adams? He obviously wasn't going to stop being the man he was. She'd been a fool to think she could sway him with a few romantic walks in the woods and some good food. What if she was little more than a brief distraction?

Still, part of her rebelled at the thought of giving up on him. It wasn't like her to ignore a challenge. Even when that challenge made her feel the same frightened panic as when she'd overheard her father regret that he'd ever had a family? Those words were burned into her six-year-old psyche. Even though she'd fought to rise above the harsh sentiment, despite dedicating herself to all things good and fun and romantic and fantastic, her father's scorn was always in the back of her mind.

Shane didn't have her coping skills. He'd spent much of his adult life shutting down his emotions. He might never be open to love. Could she live with that?

She recalled his text in the wake of her career tailspin after learning Camilla Maxwell was going to become the hotel's romance concierge. We need to talk. Had they ever had the conversation he initiated? She'd hijacked the discussion with what Tom had told her. What had followed had involved lots of amazing sex and that dreamy isolation all new lovers fall into.

So, what had he intended to discuss with her?

Shane strolled into The Opulence's lobby to get a fresh cup of coffee. He'd lost track of how much caffeine he'd consumed since arriving at the hotel last night. Matt Richmond was en route to the hotel to survey the situation, but in the meantime, the staff was dealing with their anxious guests and trying to ensure that word got out to those who hadn't yet arrived that the whole retreat had been canceled.

The mood among the guests had brightened as the storm moved on, aided by the impromptu concert being given by Jessie Humphrey. The star sat at the piano, running through her vast repertoire, her gorgeous voice filling the lobby with tales of big love and excruciating loss. As the lyrics flowed over him, Shane mulled over what had occurred over the last couple of weeks that had led to the changes currently taking place in his perception.

The catalyst for his transformation stood near a pillar, listening with all her heart to Jessie Humphrey. Shane headed her way. The expression on her face was so beautiful that his heart flipped in his chest. He simply couldn't wait another second to tell her the impact she'd made on his life.

"Listen," he began, stopping beside her. "About earlier."

She shook her head vigorously. "Not now. I'm in the

best place I could be right at the moment. This is my favorite song of Jesse's. I just want to listen to her sing."

Shane noted this bit of data into the mental file where he cataloged Isabel's favorite things. Never before had he paid such keen attention to what a woman wanted or needed. Isabel was different. She did so much for everyone else. He wanted to return the favor. To create special moments for her. So, instead of intruding, he stood beside her, resisting the urge to seek physical contact, and listened with his heart wide open.

When applause broke out at the end of the song, Isabel turned to him. "Last night you didn't give me a chance to explain." Beneath her calm, reasonable tone was a thread of pain. "You didn't give me a chance to get a word in edgewise. Instead you just went on and on about how horrible it was that I might be pregnant, insinuating that you might be forced to have me in your life longer than you'd anticipated."

"That's not what I meant at all."

Isabel shook her head, not letting him sidestep with excuses. "I'm not a fool. I know real panic when I see it. You can handle anything that gets thrown at you in your career, but one broken condom…" Her words came quickly as angry color rushed into her cheeks. She sucked in a breath and let it out slowly. "One broken condom sends you into a tailspin."

Shane resented the depiction of his reaction, but she deserved to be angry. For several seconds he'd been blind with panic. "I'm sorry," he said. This was being in a relationship. Listening and respect. "You had something to say. I didn't give you the chance."

"I didn't freak out." She crossed her arms over her chest and jut out her chin, wordlessly challenging whether he was ready to hear her out. "Because I'm not going to get pregnant."

A familiar worry rose in him, but pushed it down. He couldn't react to data and make decisions without considering how it might emotionally impact the next person. He needed to hear her out and discuss what was bothering him.

"How is it that you know?"

"Because I'm on the pill. I have been for years. I have heavy periods and became anemic because of them. The doctors recommended birth control." She assessed his reaction through narrowed eyes. "I'll spare you the explanation how that works."

Shane decided most men would be uncomfortable when confronted by talk of periods and bleeding so he kept his response to an understanding nod.

"I probably should've said something early on," she continued, "but we didn't know each other that well and condoms are always a good idea."

Utilizing nonverbal cues to communicate that he was following her was the perfect decision. Better that he not speak until he was clear what would make him sound intelligent and supportive.

"So you don't have to worry." She paused, and her grief struck him like a bat to the gut. "Because I know what a big deal that would be for you. It would just destroy your life."

Although her inflection hadn't changed, her words told him that his behavior had damaged her trust. And he suspected that he'd have to go to great lengths to repair it.

"It would change my life," he agreed, taking her hand, relieved when she didn't pull free. "But I'd be open to it."

"Since when?" she grumbled. Hope flickered in her eyes and was quickly extinguished.

"You put a spell on me," he said.

"That's…" She looked nonplussed. "I wasn't trying to."

"Weren't you?" He'd thought about this long and hard. "Your whole plan was to make me fall in love with you. The marketing strategy was nothing but a ploy."

She gaped at him for several seconds before sputtering, "That's not true." But the way her gaze dodged away from his said there was more to it than that.

"You played like you were appealing to my business side because if you'd told me that you were out to seduce me, I would've run like hell." He paused to offer her a chance to deny it. "Right?"

"Me, seduce you?" She laughed. "As if I could."

After everything that had happened between them, she really had no sense of her appeal. "Why would you doubt how much I want you?"

"You made it pretty clear you thought I needed to broaden my horizons. I knew I wasn't the sort of sophisticated woman you're used to." As if suddenly aware that they were holding hands, she tried to tug free.

Shane tightened his hold and brought their clasped hands to his chest. "So, what did you think we were doing?"

"I guess I thought it was a fling while you were in the area for the Richmond retreat." She stared at his chin. "I mean, you were pretty clear about your priorities."

He wasn't sure he was fully buying her claim of a fling. Then again, it hadn't occurred to Shane until that moment that Isabel might not feel as strongly about him as he did about her. After all, the reason she'd been angry with him once before had been due to Tom's handling of the romance concierge situation. That time, Shane had thought she was mad because he hadn't called her after their first time together.

"Then why did you get angry at how I reacted to the condom breaking?"

She gave an exasperated sigh. "Because I thought you'd just drift out of my life. Stop calling. That I could've handled. Watching a man panic at the thought of having gotten her pregnant is not any woman's idea of a great way to end an evening."

"Is that what you want?" As he asked the question, white-hot agony invaded his chest. "For me to drift out of your life? Stop calling?"

"Of course not." She stared at their clasped hands. "But maybe where we are now is a good place to call it quits."

She was giving him an out. All he had to do was agree and they could part as friends. He could go back to business as usual. Long hours. Lots of travel. Eating alone.

The lifestyle he'd embraced because he wanted to prove his dad wrong. Stupid. He shouldn't care what that sorry excuse for a parental authority thought about him. Shane took in the woman standing before him, remembering all the times her gaze had reflected joy and passion and respect for him. Did he really believe there was a better mirror in the world than Isabel's gorgeous hazel eyes?

"I don't want to call it quits," he growled, throat seizing at the thought of ever losing her. "Not now. Not ever."

A tear caught on her lashes as she glanced up at him. "Don't say it unless you mean it," she whispered. "I couldn't take it."

Not giving a damn who saw, he swept his arm around her waist and brought her tight against him. Cupping her cheek, he brought his lips to hers and kissed her with all his heart and soul. She made a sound like a sob and opened herself to him. Joy radiated from her, flooding his senses. Pieces clicked into place inside him. He was whole for the first time in forever.

Filled with absolute peace and belonging, he broke off the kiss and nuzzled her ear. "I love you."

She jerked back and raked his expression with her doubts. After several rapid heartbeats, disbelief morphed into astonishment.

"You do," she murmured, placing her palm against his cheek. "You really do. I love you, too. I've been falling for you for a year. I just never imagined..." Her words faded into a husky chuckle. "You love me."

"How could I not? Thanks to you I no longer want to bury myself in work and avoid the things that could truly make me happy, like you and our future together.

I may not always be comfortable sharing my emotions, but you are the perfect woman to help me with that."

"But, Shane, after all the time and energy you've put into building your career with Richmond Hotel Group, can you just decide to have a personal life?"

He saw the point she was trying to make and the reassurance she needed. "I've given enough to the company. I want to make time for myself. For us."

"Us," she repeated, her smile blooming. "I really like the sound of that."

"So, how do we begin our new life together?"

"I have some vacation time I still need to use up before the end of the year," she said. "Maybe I can come to Seattle and we can play house for a week. I'll be your fifties housewife, waiting at home to greet you, wearing a flowered apron and carrying chilled martinis."

"Or you could pick your top fantasy destination and we could go there."

Wonder bloomed on Isabel's face, causing Shane's heart to pound. Making her happy was going to become a top priority for him. Now he understood why she took such satisfaction from giving other people their dream moments. The joy came right back.

"You'd do that for me?" She wrapped herself around his arm, giddy with delight. "You'd take time off?"

"I'd do that for us." He dipped his head and kissed her lips. "We're a team from now on. I just want to make you happy."

She slid her fingers into his hair and held him close. "You already do."

Epilogue

Teresa recoiled from Liam's displeasure. What had gone wrong? His tight gaze raked over her face, leading her to suspect something had blown up and he distrusted her again. How could he do this to her after last night? Was he regretting giving her a glimpse into his troubled past? In the cold light of day, was the vulnerability too much for him to bear?

As if in slow motion, she could see what was coming. He was poised to take it all back. To push her away. To reject their intimacy. To retreat into skepticism and doubt.

This time, she was not having it. She could not bear to have Liam toss her aside again. He didn't get to hold all the cards. To dictate the ebb and flow of their relationship. To give and withhold affection because he was angry or hurt or suspicious. To take her needs and emotions for granted.

Hiding her pain and longing behind annoyance, she held up her hand. "Let me start. You don't have to say a word, Liam. Last night was crazy. We connected on a new level, but that doesn't mean it's going anywhere." As she shrugged offhandedly, Teresa knew she was giving the greatest performance of her life. "We're good in bed together and as fun as it's been, I'm really not looking for more."

Liam's eyes widened as her words landed. This was clearly not the reaction he'd anticipated and shutters slammed down over his expression. Obviously he wasn't relieved that she'd beaten him to the punch. No doubt she'd dented his pride. Teresa felt a sick rush of satisfaction followed almost immediately by despair. This wasn't her. She didn't save her dignity by making situations worse. She fixed problems. Made people feel joy and delight.

Still, a hint of uncertainty made her second-guess her reaction. Wouldn't she have done a better job of handling things if she'd let him have his say before throwing their fledgling romance under the bus?

Her phone buzzed and, hoping it was her brother trying to reach out to her again, Teresa glanced down at the screen. To her dismay, the message was from Corrine and carried an urgency she couldn't ignore.

911

Grinding her teeth in irritation at being interrupted during a key moment of personal discovery and transformation, Teresa nevertheless couldn't resist the pull of responsibility. She keyed up the message and stared at the link Corrine had shared.

The headline stopped her breath.

MOGUL'S TORRID AFFAIR WITH FATHER'S MISTRESS ENDS AFTER HER SURPRISE INHERITANCE REVEALED.

"Did you do this?" She held up her phone so Liam could read the screen. From his lack of surprise, she realized this is what he'd come to talk to her about. "No, this isn't your style," she corrected herself. "But you think I was somehow involved."

"I saw you talking to Nicolette Ryan."

Her first impulse was to explain that part of her job involved coordinating with reporters who were covering newsworthy events like the Richmond retreat.

"You know what, I don't have time for this. You think I'm untrustworthy, but I think you're afraid that we were starting to make a connection." Distantly Teresa realized that her impassioned words contradicted the declaration she'd made seconds earlier about it being all hot sex and nothing more between them. "Intimacy scares the hell out of you because you don't like feeling exposed and out of control. Well, that's your stuff to deal with. I'm done trying to prove myself to you. From here on out, the only contact I want to have with you is about my shares in Christopher Corporation."

And with that, she pivoted on her heel and walked

away before he glimpsed the hot tears that flooded her eyes, turning her world into an indistinguishable, uncertain mess.

* * * * *

How will Liam and Teresa deal with this latest news?
Is Joshua in trouble?
Will Jessie's performance go on as planned?

Don't miss a single episode in the
Dynasties: Secrets of the A-List quartet!

Book One
Tempted by Scandal *by Karen Booth*

Book Two
Taken by Storm *by Cat Schield*
Available June 2019

Book Three
Seduced by Second Chances *by Reese Ryan*
Available July 2019

Book Four
Redeemed by Passion *by Joss Wood*
Available August 2019

Get 4 FREE REWARDS!

We'll send you 2 FREE Books plus 2 FREE Mystery Gifts.

Harlequin® Desire books feature heroes who have it all: wealth, status, incredible good looks... everything but the right woman.

FREE Value Over **$20**

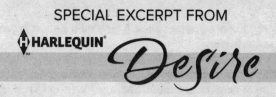
*When Reid Singleton buys the beautiful stranger
a drink, he doesn't realize she's actually his best friend's
little sister, Drew Fleming—until after he sleeps with
her! Will their fledgling relationship survive…as even
bigger family secrets threaten to derail everything?*

Read on for a sneak peek at
One Night, White Lies
by Jessica Lemmon!

London-born Reid Singleton didn't know a damn thing about
women's shoes. So when he became transfixed by a pair on
the dance floor, fashion wasn't his dominating thought.

They were pink, but somehow also metallic, with long
Grecian-style straps crisscrossing delicate, gorgeous ankles.
He curled his scotch to his chest and backed into the shadows,
content to watch the woman who owned those ankles for a
bit.

From those pinkish metallic spikes, the picture only
improved. He followed the straps to perfectly rounded calves
and the outline of tantalizing thighs lost in a skirt that moved
when she did. The cream-colored skirt led to a sparkling
gold top. Her shoulders were slight, the swells of her breasts
snagging his attention for a beat, and her hair fell in curls over
those small shoulders. Dark hair with a touch of mahogany, or
maybe rich cherry. Not quite red, but with a notable amount
of warmth.

HDEXP0619

He sipped from his glass, again taking in the skirt, both flirty and fun in equal measures. A guy could get lost in there. Get lost in her.

An inviting thought, indeed.

The brunette spun around, her skirt swirling, her smile a seemingly permanent feature. She was lively and vivid, and even in her muted gold-and-cream ensemble, somehow the brightest color in the room. A man approached her, and Reid promptly lost his smile, a strange feeling of propriety rolling over him and causing him to bristle.

The suited man was average height with a receding hairline. He was on the skinny side, but the vision in gold simply smiled up at him, dazzling the man like she'd cast a spell. When she shook her head in dismissal and the man ducked his head and moved on, relief swamped Reid, but he still didn't approach her.

Careful was the only way to proceed, or so instinct told him. She was open but somehow skittish, in an outfit he couldn't take his eyes from. He hadn't been in a rush to approach the goddess like some of the other men in the room.

Reid had already decided to carefully choose his moment, but as she made eye contact, he realized he wasn't going to have to approach her.

She was coming to him.

One Night, White Lies
by Jessica Lemmon,
available July 2019 wherever
Harlequin® Desire books and ebooks are sold.

www.Harlequin.com

HDEXP0619